The Best of Animals

THE BEST OF ANIMALS

——— *stories* ———

LAUREN GRODSTEIN

A Karen and Michael Braziller Book

PERSEA BOOKS / NEW YORK

Persea Books, Inc.
853 Broadway
New York, NY 10003

"Family Vacation" and "Such a Pretty Face" originally appeared
in *Virgin Fiction 2* and *Ontario Review,* respectively.

Library of Congress Cataloging-in-Publication Data

Grodstein, Lauren.
The best of animals : stories / by Lauren Grodstein
p. cm.
ISBN 0-89255-281-6 (alk. paper)
1. United States—Social Life and customs—20th century—Fiction. 2. Young
adults—Fiction. I. Title.
PS3607.R63 B47 2002
813'.6—dc21
2001036859

Design by Rita Lascaro
Typeset in Goudy

For my mother and father,
Jessie and Elliot

But he who is unable to live in society, or who has no need because he is sufficient for himself, must be either a beast or a god: he is no part of a state. A social instinct is implanted in all men by nature . . . For man, when perfected, is the best of animals.

—Aristotle, Politics

Contents

The Best of Animals

Lonely Planet

I DREAMED LAST NIGHT about having Richard Gere's baby.
Curious, because I've never considered myself a big
Richard Gere fan. I mean, sure, I did have a few tender
thoughts about him after *Pretty Woman*. And I remember
catching a glimpse of his butt on cable when I was a little
girl, and looking on with fascination until my mother
caught me and sent me to bed. But it was only years later
that I realized that the butt I saw was Richard Gere's and
that the movie must have been *An Officer and a Gentleman*.
And right now, thinking about it—I can't even *name* any
other Richard Gere movies. Not a single one. Although it
is true that I get him confused with Warren Beatty—I did
see *Ishtar* and I think that might have been Richard Gere
in it.

No, wait, forget it. Warren Beatty.

Anyway, in my dream, our baby didn't have a name. I'm not even sure if our baby had a specific gender. It was just a baby, with big blue eyes and a round bald head and Richard was very kind to it, very gentle. In my dream I was supposed to take Richard and the baby to my mother's house for a Passover seder, but Richard didn't want to go. It wasn't because a Passover seder conflicted with his well-publicized Buddhist beliefs; it was just that he didn't love me enough to accompany me and our baby to my mother's house. He claimed he had some big Hollywood thing to go to and that was that. In my dream, I was very understanding.

At my mother's house people said, "Where's Richard? Where's Richard?" My aunt Sylvia who's been dead for three years said, "I thought you were gonna bring the big shot Richard Gere. Here's your baby. Where's Richard?"

I said, "He didn't love me enough to come, I guess."

Aunt Sylvia said, "Always feeling sorry for yourself," and the baby started to cry in my arms.

When I woke up this morning I shook my head and tried to forget that Richard Gere had broken my heart. I walked down the street to buy a bagel and some coffee, which I buy every morning, and also *Entertainment Weekly* magazine, which I'd never bought before. But I thought I might find an article on Richard Gere or, if not, that the magazine might have some other news that would distract me.

"Morning, Julie," said Luis, who worked at the bodega on the corner and pronounced my name "Yoo-lee."

"Morning, Luis," I said. "The usual, and also *Entertainment Weekly*."

"No problem," Luis said. Luis was a very short man with slick black hair and bright brown eyes. I once thought he was in love with me, simply because it was an amusing thing to think about. My bagel and coffee and magazine came to five dollars and forty-nine cents, which was almost as much money as I had on me, and as I walked to the subway on Fourteenth Street and Seventh Avenue I thought to myself that maybe I should see fewer movies.

In the office, Denise in the next cubicle was talking on the phone to her child. "Lucille—" she whispered sternly. "Lucille, you have to go to school today. That's it. I don't care what Nana says."

I suppose she was whispering because she didn't want our boss, Janet, to know that she was making a personal phone call, but Janet had kids of her own and was a very understanding woman. I didn't know what Denise was so afraid of.

She slammed down the phone. "That child is doing her best to drive me crazy."

"I know," I said. "Last night I dreamed I had Richard Gere's baby."

Denise gave me a queer look and sipped her coffee.

I thought that Lucille was a strange name for a child because it sounded so old-fashioned, so grandmotherly. I knew that old-fashioned names were trendy among young parents, that hip people liked to name their kids things like Charles and Lillian and Maxwell. I supposed that this was a perfectly innocent trend, except among certain people who took it too far. There was no reason, for instance, to name your child Milo or Millicent.

These were both names my sister was considering for her baby, due in April. Millicent Feinbaum. Poor kid.

I turned on my computer and adjusted the monitor so that it would face me directly. I was supposed to work on one of the projects for the new campaign, but I didn't feel like it. Instead, I looked at the picture taped to the side of my computer. It was a photo of me and Allan, taken when we were in college, looking a little bit younger and much happier. Allan left three months ago to go explore the Amazon with a backpack full of bug spray and *Lonely Planet* guides. He was not my boyfriend, but I liked to pretend he was.

Just before he left, I asked if I could keep one of his T-shirts and smell it when he wasn't around. He said, "Sure, if that's what you want. Take the blue one. I don't wear it all that much." I took the blue one and I also took a green one with a Jets logo on it because I knew for a fact that Allan was a Giants fan and wouldn't miss it. I've been sleeping in the blue one and wearing the Jets one to the gym. I often wonder, on the Stairmaster, if Allan is thinking about me.

When he broke up with his girlfriend Dorie, Allan called me on the phone, drunk. He said that he dialed my number because he really wanted to call Dorie but knew that he shouldn't. I said, "Sure, I understand."

Then he said he was at O'Hanlon's down by First Avenue and would I please come because he was so drunk he wasn't sure if he would make it home all right. It was almost midnight. I said of course I would, no problem, and put on my lipstick in a good shade of pink and also my high-heeled leather boots, which I bought myself for my birthday, and I brushed my hair. With my hair down I looked a little bit like Dorie, although she was taller. I thought that if I looked like Dorie, that might cheer Allan up.

When I arrived at O'Hanlon's, Allan was sitting on a stool with his head on the bar.

"Julie," he slurred when he saw me. "Thank you, thank you . . . "

Allan had asked Dorie to marry him at one point, and she'd said she'd think about it. Then she never got back to him, and he was too nervous to bring up the subject again. When she dumped him, he still had a ring hidden in his sock drawer.

"You don't have to thank me, Allan," I said, and took a seat next to him at the bar. "Guinness, please," I said to the bartender. "And one for my friend here."

"I don't think your friend needs any more, lady," the bartender said. "Anyway, he's drinking scotch."

"Fine," I said. "Another scotch."

"Julie—" Allan crooned in a drunken manner. "Ju-u-u-lie . . . "

"It's okay, Allan," I said. "I'm getting you another drink."

I put my purse on the bar and fished out my cigarettes, and when the bartender slid my Guinness toward me I blew a puff of smoke in his face. "Thank you, sir," I said.

"Thank you," the bartender said, not bothering to wave the smoke away.

I tapped my cigarette in the ashtray and flipped my hair around so that it would curl over my shoulder seductively.

"So, Allan," I said, clinking my Guinness against his scotch glass. "Here's to you."

He didn't respond.

"Here's to you," I said again.

"I'm not drinking," he slurred. "I'm drunk. I need to go home."

"Don't be a candy-ass, Allan," I encouraged. "Don't be a fruit." His head was still down and I thought I saw a little drool escape from his lips and form a puddle on the bar. I reached in and wiped it up with a cocktail napkin. "Come on," I said. "You're not getting any younger."

Allan lifted his head and winced. "I've been drinking—" he said, and rubbed his left eye. "I've been drinking all night."

"I can tell." He looked a mess. Half his hair was matted against the side of his face and the other half was standing straight on end. His shirt was stained with sweat and beer, and his eyes, usually so clear and green, were red and mostly closed. When we were in college Allan rarely drank. He would come visit me or pick me up to go to the library and if I smelled like beer or vodka, he'd make a face. I was relieved when he finally started drinking too, so that I'd no longer have to hide my own fondness for the occasional Guinness. It was good to see him drunk.

I took a sip and said, "I think I actually saw Dorie on the subway yesterday."

Allan rubbed his left eye again and sat up a little straighter. His neck was blotchy. "You're kidding," he said. "You're kidding."

"Not kidding," I said. "I think it was her. And I hate to tell you this, Allan, but she was with some guy, and he had his arm around her."

"What?" Allan said, his eyes snapping open. "Are you sure?"

"Well, it's hard to say anything for sure," I said. "But it did look like her, you know, with the haircut. I didn't say anything because I thought it would be awkward."

"You're sure he had his arm around her?"

"What am I, blind?" I asked. "I know what I saw."

"Julie," he said, leaning in toward me. His breath was just awful. "I need you to be sure."

"Okay, then," I said, and tapped my cigarette. "I'm sure."

"Fucking bitch!" Allan exploded, slamming his fists on the bar. It was a sort of dramatic gesture coming from a man who moments before had seemed half-conscious; the other customers turned and stared at us for a moment before returning to their own business. I was embarrassed for Allan for making a scene. "Bitch," he said again, a little more softly, and put his head back down on the bar.

I had never liked Dorie all that much, although I tried. But she always seemed to have this attitude with me, and when I saw a girl who looked just like her on the subway giggling and laughing with this other guy, I thought to myself, what a bitch. What a bitch to go and do that to a great guy like Allan, to a wonderful gem of a young man like my friend Allan. On the subway, I said, "Hey, Dorie!" but she didn't look up. The subway is crowded, though. People don't always hear you.

Allan lifted up his head again and took a swig of his

scotch and then started coughing loudly. "Easy there, cow-boy," I said. "No need to take it down all in one shot."

"How could she—how could she . . . " His neck was even blotchier, and I could tell it was hard for him to get the words out. "It hasn't even been four weeks. Not even four weeks, the fucking bitch."

"She *was* a bitch, Allan," I said. "I'll say it again: you're better off without her."

Allan nodded sullenly. It's hard to watch people when they're suffering from heartbreak. "You know," he said, "I never knew what she wanted. I tried to be there for her, I tried to be everything for her, but sometimes you just give and you give and she doesn't want to take it, you know? You can't force someone like Dorie to take."

"I know," I said, and touched his hand, because it was so sad to see him this way and I wanted to offer some comfort. "I know."

He finished his scotch and ordered another. He seemed to be a little bit livelier now, and even made some joke with the bartender about all women being cunts. It was a smoky bar, an old-time Irish pub like the kind they have a lot of on the east end of Fourteenth Street. It was full of people who seemed like they'd lost their jobs years ago and never found the energy to get new ones. I was one of maybe three women in the place, and certainly the only one with blown-out hair and great new boots. I was also wearing my gold chain-link bracelet and the watch my father bought me from Cartier when I got my job at the firm. At O'Hanlon's on a Wednesday night, I was a babe.

By two in the morning, Allan almost seemed alive. He had vanished to the bathroom several times, maybe to puke, which usually makes a person feel better. He had wiped his hand through his hair so that it was messy all over and not just on one side. Cute.

"Do you have to go to work tomorrow?" I asked.

"I've been calling in sick," he said. "My boss thinks I might have pneumonia."

"I'm taking the day off tomorrow myself," I said. "I just decided. There's no way I can concentrate on the dog-food campaign after all this excitement."

"You're great, Julie," Allan said. I felt hot with pride.

At four in the morning O'Hanlon's closed and the bartender kicked us out. "Where do we go now?" I asked.

The street was dark and empty except for a homeless guy lying on top of a subway grate. O'Hanlon's green-lit sign flickered and went black, and I took Allan's hand.

"I think I better go home," he said, his voice wobbly, his legs also wobbly. "I think I better find a cab. It's cold out."

"Are you going to make it by yourself?" I asked. "You seem a little unsteady."

"Yeah," he said. He didn't let go of my hand. "Yeah, I'll be fine."

"You know what?" I said. I wasn't tired and I still wanted to be helpful. "You know what? I'll put you in a cab. I'll get in a cab with you and have the cab drop you off first, just to make sure you get home all right."

"Thanks, Julie," Allan said, and wobbled on his unsteady legs. "You're the greatest."

"Oh, Allan," I said, and lifted my hand to hail us a cab. Cabs are always easy to find, even at four in the morning. You can't get a drink, but you can still score a ride.

Allan lived on Delancey Street, which was certainly out of my way, but I felt like a good person for keeping my arm around him and making sure he was okay. He fell asleep in the back of the cab, his mouth open, making faint snoring sounds. "Three twenty-five Delancey," I told the driver and straightened Allan's collar in the back seat.

Ten minutes later the cab pulled to a stop. "I think I should walk you up," I said.

"We're here?" Allan opened his eyes, but barely.

"Come on," I said. "I'm walking you up."

Allan lived on the third floor and needless to say there was no elevator, so after fumbling with his keys and finally opening the door, I had to sort of drag him up the stairs with my arm around him and my leg supporting his. It was hard work. By the third floor, I was sweaty. I fumbled through his key ring again and finally found the one that let us in.

"You go lie down," I said. Allan's apartment was a single large room, fairly neat, with a kitchenette in one corner and a colorful rug on the floor. Lots of television and stereo equipment lined the wall next to the door, and a big poster of a Vargas girl hung over his bed in the opposite corner. "I'm going to freshen up." I walked Allan over to the bed, and dropped him on it, and he fell on his face with a long, noisy groan. I threw my jacket on the bed next to him and went into the bathroom.

The bathroom was small and tiled in bright yellow. I turned on the lights and looked in the mirror and was pleased to see that my hair still hung neatly and my eye makeup wasn't too smudged. There was only one toothbrush in the toothbrush holder; I picked it up and took the Crest out of the vanity case and brushed my teeth until my mouth tasted minty and sweet. Then I took off my sweater and my boots, my gray stretch pants, my trouser socks. I folded them neatly on the toilet seat and then thought about it for a second and decided also to remove my new La Perla bra, even though it was an attractive one. I didn't think that Allan was in any state to try and remove a bra.

I turned off the bathroom lights and went back into the main room. Allan was snoring, fully dressed, on the bed. I sat down next to him.

"Allan?" I said. "Allan?" I shook him slightly, but he didn't wake up. "Allan?"

"Julie?" he mumbled, and rolled over so that he was lying on his back. I touched his face, and then his neck. He looked so sweaty and uncomfortable. I decided to unbutton his shirt, just the top button at first, but then I thought about it and decided to unbutton the whole thing. The shirt smelled like rotten eggs, and I thought that it was probably unsanitary to fall asleep in such a stained and sweaty garment. I threw it across the room, and it landed on top of the television. Allan's chest was pasty and a little soft-looking, and his nipples had fine brown hairs around them. They matched the hair on his head. I thought he was lovely.

"Julie," he mumbled again, and sort of took an affectionate swipe at my shoulders. His eyes were still closed, though, and he ended up hitting my breast. It didn't hurt. "Let me sleep," he said.

"Well, you're kind of a mess, Allan," I said. "You shouldn't sleep in these sweaty clothes." I wondered if he could tell how seductive I was being. He mumbled something and put his arm over his eyes. "The lights."

"Oh, sure," I said. I should have thought of that first thing. I got up and turned off the lights and parted the drapes a little so some moonlight would brighten the room. I tiptoed back over to the bed, where Allan was making heavy phlegmy snoring noises. With the drapes open, I could see him perfectly. There was a big blotchy beer stain on the left leg of his Dockers. They had to come off.

He didn't resist much as I unbuckled his belt and carefully removed his pants. Truth be told, he was snoring so loudly I don't even think he heard his zipper unzip. Then he lay there in just his blue socks and Snoopy boxer shorts—a little ridiculous. I took off his socks, one by one. I wanted to wash his feet, but I thought that might disturb him.

Then I just sat up, looking at his soft body, his belly covered in light brown hairs rising gently above the elastic band of his boxer shorts. He looked like a little boy.

I reached down and touched the hair on his belly, following the line of it as it grew thicker and darker and then disappeared behind the white fabric of his shorts. I touched it softly, up and down, hoping that my touch would provide him with a warm, tickling sensation. He didn't even seem to notice, though. Just kept on snoring.

I felt under the elastic of his shorts, just with my index finger at first and then, slowly, with my whole hand. I slid my hand in and felt the thickness of his pubic hair, tightly curled, wound up like springs. Amazing to think of all that was hidden down there. I kept reaching, gently, softly. I touched his penis.

Probably due to the alcohol and the late hour it felt like a soft, sweet little thing, not much bigger than a thumb, really, and as smooth and velvety as calfskin. I squeezed it between my fingers and then, deciding I wanted a better look, I pulled down his boxer shorts with my free hand. They stuck a little as I tried to get them over his hips, but with a forceful tug, they came on down.

I examined him the way a mother would examine a child after an accident, lifting it up, getting down close to it, touching it softly to feel for bumps or scars. It was small, but it seemed perfect. I put my tongue to it. It tasted fine.

I wondered if, somewhere in his dreams, Allan knew how close I was to his most private self and was pleased. I wondered if he was sorry that he was so drunk and so tired and that we couldn't make love. Maybe he was dreaming that I was Dorie. Maybe he was glad that I wasn't. Maybe, I thought, if I just tried a little, he would become aroused and want to make love to me. I kissed his penis, softly at first, and then harder. I put my mouth around it. Nothing happened.

Realizing that I needed to take drastic measures to stiffen Allan up, so to speak, I took off my own underwear and sat on top of him, grinding down gently onto his groin, hoping the pressure would make him aroused. No such luck. But it felt pretty nice to be grinding on top of him anyway, with his soft naked body under me in the moonlight, and so I rocked back and forth on top of him for a good several minutes until I didn't need to rock anymore and fell next to him on the bed, happy.

"Julie," he mumbled a minute or two later. "Hmmrrrph . . . " He rolled over and his arm fell over me, which was nice. Like we were cuddling. I closed my eyes and we lay there like that for a while, but the truth was I was stuck in a sort of uncomfortable position and Allan was breathing hard on me, his breath still putrid. I wished I could brush his teeth. I pushed his arm off me and sat up and was going to go get the toothbrush to try and brush his teeth when I realized it was impossible. I'd never get him to keep his mouth open.

But as long as I was up and wide awake I thought I might as well take a look around the apartment. I didn't mean to be nosy, but Allan and I had been fairly good friends for years and anyway, we had practically just made love. I wanted to know what he hid inside his apartment. I wondered if he kept pictures of Dorie, or of me.

His dresser was located near the kitchenette, the way dressers sometimes are in one-room apartments. On top of the dresser were two framed photographs; I picked them up and took them over to the window. One was of Allan and his friends Greg and Joe, two guys I knew in college and didn't like all that much. Joe and I used to sleep together, in fact, until I found out that he was also sleeping with one of my sorority sisters and saying terrible things about me to her. When I confronted him, he laughed and called me a crazy bitch. Joe. I was offended that Allan even had a picture of him and would have dropped it out the window but knew that such an act really wasn't within my rights.

The other photograph, cheaply framed, was of Allan and Dorie in black-tie clothing, holding champagne glasses. The bottom of the picture was printed with white lettering: "Boxtree New Year's Gala." Boxtree was the computer consulting firm Allan worked for. Dorie's dress showed way too much cleavage.

I sat down on the leather chair by the window to really examine the picture. It was strange to be naked with Dorie's face smiling up at me, strange in the same way it is to go to the bathroom while reading a magazine and seeing a photo of a gorgeous model smiling up at you while you're trying not to be constipated. I felt sort of embarrassed. I grabbed a T-shirt off Allan's floor and put it on.

Allan looked happy in the picture, or happy at first glance, but the more I looked at him the more I could see he was troubled. His eyes, usually so sparkly, seemed reddish and faint. He was smiling perhaps too widely, the smile of someone who's trying to hide his inner discontent. His bow tie was off-center, his cummerbund too low. A man truly satisfied with his woman would be more meticulous about his appearance in order to please her.

Dorie herself, in a dress that I could just tell was bought on sale, too much thigh and too much eyeshadow, like a mid-priced hooker—well, I couldn't believe Allan had wasted all that time on her. And that he still kept her picture on his dresser. Poor sap.

I returned to the dresser to put back the photos and was happy to feel Allan's T-shirt swaying around my hips. Swinging my butt around a little, just to feel the fabric over it, I imagined that I was Dorie. What would it be like to wear Allan's T-shirts all the time, to feel entitled to them? What would it be like to see him naked whenever I wanted, to have his arms around me whenever, to sleep in this room every night? What would it be like to always have him all to myself? I sighed and repositioned the photographs on top of the dresser. I opened up his top drawer. Boxers and socks.

But I knew what else was in there.

Behind rolls of thick cotton sport socks, hidden all the way in the back, sat a little velvet box. I removed it carefully and closed the drawer, trying to be as quiet as possible. I took the box to the chair in the moonlight. I sat down.

Allan was lying opposite me; he had rolled over again so that he faced the chair. His mouth was slightly open, but his snoring had grown softer. I imagined that he was somehow conscious of what I was doing, though, and sort of pleased. I mean, I wasn't stupid—I knew he was fast asleep and snoring—but I also thought that maybe karmically, maybe in his dreams somewhere, he knew what I was up to. And so when I opened the box to find a lovely diamond solitaire, I didn't feel the least bit guilty. I felt like Allan approved. When I took the ring out and held it up in the moonlight, it sparkled, the way a good diamond ring will.

I bent down and kissed Allan on the cheek and then went back to the bathroom and turned on the lights. Standing under the hot bright fluorescents, I tried to slide his ring onto my index finger. It was a tight fit. But I was wearing his T-shirt and his ring and I felt like I was home. I thought for a moment that if I closed my eyes and wished with all my might, then Allan might wake up and see me, see how perfect I looked in his clothing and his apartment. He would understand, karmically speaking, how much I belonged exactly where I was. Then I would have his children, and they would have his green eyes, and we could name them anything.

Millicent or Milo. I would make such a good mother.

I closed the bathroom door and sat down on the toilet seat and covered the ring on my left finger with my right hand, squeezed my right hand tightly over my left one, touched the ring and tried to convince myself that it belonged to me. What if it were mine? Couldn't it be mine? And if I took it, if I took it and wore it forever, well, wouldn't it then become mine? Would Allan ever notice?

I realized then that I was crying—that I was crying because I knew the answer. I couldn't have the ring. I could do whatever I wanted with Allan in the dark, but the ring just wasn't mine.

I must have fallen asleep. With the sun bright in my face, Allan woke me by gently tapping me on the shoulder. His breath smelled sweet. "Julie," he said. "Julie, wake up."

I was on the floor, on the brightly colored rug.

"Allan?" He had showered and dressed in a blue T-shirt and jeans, his hair damped down on his forehead.

"We need to talk," he said.

"Oh," I sat up and rubbed my eyes and realized I was still wearing the ring. I quickly dropped my hands.

"I think—" he sat down on the floor, opposite me, and touched my knee. "I think something happened last night."

"Happened?" I asked. His expression was so serious.

"I think we might have—we might have—well, the truth is I was so drunk that I really don't remember what happened, but I woke up naked, and—well, your clothing was in the bathroom."

I nodded. "What time is it?"

"Almost one in the afternoon," he said. He didn't let go of my knee. "Julie, I just want you to know that whatever happened—"

"Oh, forget it, Allan," I said. "We were drunk."

"—that I'm sorry."

I nodded again. I needed to get the ring off without him noticing.

"I never meant to take advantage of you," he continued, still looking so damn serious. "You've been a great friend for almost five years and it kills me to think that I got so drunk that I hurt you. I really am sorry."

"Don't be sorry," I said, suddenly annoyed. "What's to be sorry about?" I held my hands up in front of my face and started tugging at the ring on my finger.

"What's that?" Allan asked, taking his hand off my knee. "Is that Dorie's engagement ring?"

"Just forget it, Allan."

"What are you doing wearing my ring?"

"If you don't even remember last night, I don't think you should be asking me that question."

"What?"

"Forget it," I said. "Help me get this fucking thing off."

Allan stood up, wide-eyed and nervous. He took a jar of Vaseline off the windowsill and handed it to me. "I don't get it," he said, flustered.

"Well, I don't want to talk about it."

"Okay," he said, pathetic and nervous. "Okay."

I rubbed my finger with the Vaseline and the ring slid off as smoothly as if it had never been there in the first place. "I've got to go."

"Okay," he said again, still flustered. Well, good, then. I didn't really give a shit how flustered Allan was. I went to the bathroom and put on my pants and boots and grabbed the rest of my stuff and jammed it into my bag. I was furious, furious that he looked so serious, furious that he was so sorry, furious that he didn't notice how beautiful I looked in his fucking ring.

Allan was waiting for me outside the bathroom door. "Julie—" he started, but I waved my hand at him and hurried out, angry and, for some reason, ashamed.

We made up eventually. Over the next few weeks, he left several apologetic messages on my machine, and when I finally picked up the phone to talk, he told me that he was leaving for the Amazon. He said he needed some time to reconstruct his life.

"In the Amazon?" I asked.

"Well," he said, "at least I'll be too far away to hurt anybody."

So I went over to Delancey to help him pack and that's when I took his two T-shirts, and before I left he hugged me and apologized one more time and I told him that if he ever apologized again, I'd punch him. He thought I was kidding.

The next day, at work, I taped the picture of me and Allan to my computer. Denise who sits next to me asked if he was my man, and I told her of course he is. He hasn't been the only one, and it's not like we were ever really that close— just drinking buddies, kind of, just casual friends—but Denise thinks he's mine. And anyway, we did come close that one night, and that night was about as much as I ever expected to know of real love.

What frightens me now is that with Allan gone, I don't know too many men in New York City. I try to meet people, but men are so busy, it seems, and I always end up saying the wrong thing. My sister, seven months pregnant and giddy as an idiot, always tells me not to worry. That if I'm patient and not too desperate, the right man will come along. I try to tell her that I don't think I'll ever have the chance to have my own baby with a man I really love, but she just laughs at me and says not to be silly. She says I'm very pretty and just need to learn some patience. I'm not so sure. I want to believe her.

But I'm still thinking about Richard Gere and wondering what I did wrong.

Such a Pretty Face

IT'S BEEN THE HOTTEST JULY on record, possibly the hottest July ever. On the fifth floor of a walk up on the Upper East Side (uncomfortably Upper, decidedly East), Roberta sits in the darkness, a damp towel spread across her forehead, a damp towel on her lap. She is wearing only blue bikini underwear, on sale at Target, three bucks for a pack of five. Two fans beat hot air at her from different directions, but they are useless, an insult, the whirring blades of a convection oven. It is six-thirty in the evening and Roberta can feel her skin melt into the sticky leatherette of the couch.

"Air conditioning!" Helen wheezes. Roberta didn't hear her come in (those damn noisy, useless fans!), and covers up her chest with the towel, embarrassed. She wonders again why she gave her sister keys.

"Hello to you, too," Roberta says. "Don't you knock? Why don't you ever knock?"

"Please," Helen says. She's still wheezing; the five flights have winded her. "I've seen you naked a thousand times, if that's what you're worried about, and what else am I gonna walk in on, exactly?"

"You never know," Roberta says, standing up, turning her back to her sister. The apartment is one medium-large room, and she keeps most of her clothing in a laundry basket in the corner. She finds an old men's undershirt, slightly stained, and pulls it on.

"That's it. I'm buying you an air conditioner," Helen says. "This is ridiculous. You can't sit here in the dark all day, covered in towels. It's insane."

"You wanna pay my electricity bills?"

"I'll pay your electricity bills, I don't care," Helen says. "What's money to me?" She plops down on Roberta's futon with a sigh, and Roberta worries briefly that its wooden support slats will collapse. Helen is a big girl, five foot four and close to two hundred pounds, flesh collecting around her arms and chin, making her eyes look beadier than they would on a skinny person. Lately, it seems, Helen's been getting bigger, but she has long been known to break things just by sitting on them.

"I'm going to take a shower before we go out," Roberta says. "Sit where I was sitting. It's the coolest spot in the apartment."

"My question is, of course, why you couldn't have showered before I got here. It's bad enough I have to come pick you up to get you out of this damn apartment," Helen says, eyes narrow. "But then to get here, knowing you won't be ready, knowing you're going to take forever . . . "

"Our reservation isn't until eight," Roberta says. "Relax. We have plenty of time." She stands at the doorway of her bathroom, watching her sister adjust the two fans so that they blow directly on her face. "Oh, and happy birthday."

"Yeah," Helen says. "Happy birthday to you, too." Today, on this brutally hot day in July, Roberta and Helen turn thirty.

Roberta is a secretary at a private grammar school, and during the summers, when she should be writing her novel, she sits on her couch and reads, or does the *Times* crossword. Although she has always been the "thin one," the "pretty one," she has never liked the company of strangers and counts Helen, among other things, as her best friend. Nobody ever believes they are sisters, much less twins. Roberta is dark, with long straight hair and wide brown eyes, small nose, full mouth. She is a good three inches taller than Helen and sixty pounds lighter, a healthy size eight, with muscular legs. She runs in the park four times a week; she rollerblades; she wears cheap clothing.

Helen, on the other hand—oh, Helen. How their mother worries. She has always been pudgy; she is pale and has the sort of benign face that many fat girls have, the sort of face that people often remark would be pretty, if only. Her eyes are greenish blue. The sole feature she shares with Roberta is her nose, straight, small, freckled. But where Roberta is shy,

Helen is outgoing and vivacious, quite brilliant, Harvard Law School. On the partner track at her law firm. She lives in a beautiful apartment in Gramercy Park and has air conditioning and an elevator.

Roberta scrubs herself in the icy-cold shower, uses mint shampoo in her hair, hopes that Helen isn't sweating too badly outside. When Helen sweats, her loose but well-cut clothing starts to stick in awkward places, across her chest, behind her knees.

"Wear the short black dress," Helen commands as Roberta dresses behind a screen.

"I think it's dirty."

"You should do laundry more often," Helen says. "You're a pig."

Roberta emerges five minutes later in a white miniskirt and a black cotton top, black sandals, her hair dripping in puddles behind her.

"Ready?" Helen asks, standing. Roberta can see that sweat has indeed stained Helen's abdomen, her thighs, her gorgeous Peruvian beaded blouse.

"Ready," Roberta says, and they descend, flight by flight, into the torpid dusk.

The restaurant is snooty and French, the sort of place that Helen loves but makes Roberta nervous. The waiters all have accents and the chef sends out little tastes of foods that nobody's asked for.

"Richie said he'd meet us for drinks later," Helen offers.

"Good," Roberta says. "I haven't seen him in a while."

"Well, we've been on awkward terms," Helen says. "I think he thinks I work too much." Richie is Helen's fiancé. He's a junior associate at the law firm, a year younger than Helen and completely bald. He's one of those guys who likes to wear wacky ties and take small children to baseball games.

"You do work too much," Roberta says.

"This is true," Helen agrees. "Let's get champagne." Like magic, a waiter appears at the side of their table without noise or even a rustle of air.

"Stealthy," Helen whispers, and Roberta smiles.

The champagne is presented with much ceremony, served in crystal flutes; the bottle rests in a silver bucket on a stand next to the table. The sisters toast each other.

"To Helen."

"To Roberta."

And then, together, "On the occasion of her thirtieth birthday. Cheers."

They have been celebrating birthdays with similar toasts for several years now, since they were old enough to drink Jack Daniels behind the house in Connecticut, thirteen, fourteen summers ago. Roberta looks away for a second and thinks of sitting next to her sister on the rickety back steps, swatting mosquitoes away from their calves, pouring the whiskey into cans of Coke. When the whiskey bottle was halfway empty, Helen would start singing to herself, only humming really—but as she got drunker the songs became louder, until she was absolutely shrieking the lyrics to "Danke Schoen" and "Don't You Want Me, Baby."

At the end of the evening, when the bottle was completely empty and their parents were due to return from bridge, Helen would begin to snivel.

"I'm fat," she'd say. "And nobody's ever gonna love me."

"Oh please," Roberta would say, holding her sister in her arms. "Don't be ridiculous. You're not fat, and everybody loves you."

Then Helen would start to cry for real and dribble whiskeyed saliva on Roberta's shoulder. She cried like this most every birthday, until her twenty-third, because a few days before her twenty-third she had finally (finally!) lost her virginity in a drunken backseat wrestle with Harvey McMann, their father's accountant. How she ended up in Harvey McMann's backseat is a question that Helen still refuses to answer; however, that particular summer, instead of crying, "Nobody's ever gonna love me," she cried, "Nobody's ever gonna have sex with me again." To Helen, back then, that meant pretty much the same thing.

They order. Foie gras, langoustine ravioli, braised monk-fish with a veal jus. Confit of leeks. A bottle of expensive red, chosen by Helen, who's paying. The waiter nods briefly, mutters, "Very good," and refills their champagne goblets.

"We are in for a glorious meal."

"I know," Roberta says. "Thank you."

"There's no one I'd rather be with," Helen says.

Roberta grins, a little embarrassed. "I'm looking forward to seeing Richie," she says again.

"Yes," Helen says, arranging her napkin on her lap. "I am, too."

The wedding is in October, which is three months away. The hall has been booked, the orchestra decided on, and the invitations sent to a calligrapher. Roberta's maid-of-honor gown is a soft rose color and falls to the tops of her shoes. The neckline is cut straight across the collarbone and adorned with tiny satin flowers. She found the dress at a bridal outlet in Queens; it was the first one she tried on.

Finding a plus-sized wedding gown, however, turned out to be more challenging: Vera Wang was obviously out, the department stores had nothing above a fourteen, and even the large warehouses like Kleinfeld's didn't show anything decent beyond eighteen. After weeks of miserable searching, a sympathetic shopkeeper on Long Island told Helen and Roberta about a store in Jersey that catered to the "unconventional bride." Roberta thought of transvestites, but Helen was eager to visit. It was there, in a storefront shop in Paramus, that Helen found a straight, to-the-ankle ivory satin gown, with a long beaded jacket that swayed gently over her hips and made her look two sizes slimmer. She stood in front of a three-way mirror, something she hadn't done in years, and when the sales assistant placed a long tulle veil on her head, both she and Roberta started to cry.

"You're beautiful," Roberta said. "You could launch a thousand ships."

Helen nodded, wiped her eye, and stained her off-white satin glove with mascara.

The waiter appears to refill their glasses and then vanishes like a happy dream. "Richie has a cousin from Seattle who's going to be in the groom's party," Helen says, and her voice rises slightly, which means she is up to some mischief. She lifts her champagne glass to her mouth to conceal her smile.

"And?"

"And Richie thinks you might like him. He's an English teacher or something. I think he might even have his Ph.D."

"Is that so?" Roberta asks.

"I think he's even supposed to be cute."

Roberta nods. This is a conversation she rarely feels like having but endures periodically because Helen enjoys doing the math in her head, adding Roberta to this one, or that one, so that they all equal an even four.

"Hey," Helen says, swirling her champagne around in her glass. "Did you ever call that guy I sent your way, David? The paralegal? The one who writes plays on the side?"

"I didn't," Roberta says, quietly.

"You didn't? You didn't?" Helen laughs, a laugh that Roberta might describe as jolly, if jolliness weren't the specific domain of fat people and therefore too close for comfort. "You know," Helen continues, "half the lawyers on the Guam case have crushes on David. Had I known you wouldn't call him, I'd have handed him to someone a little more grateful."

"You knew I wouldn't call him," Roberta says.

"I did," Helen confirms, still swirling the champagne. "But I tried nevertheless."

Roberta takes a swig of her own champagne and stares down at her plate. She has tried to get Helen to understand how anxious dating makes her. In the company of strange men, she stops trusting her mouth to say the right thing or her feet to walk without tripping. The idea of being with one for an entire evening terrifies her, and she has never been the type to confront her fears head-on. She's always preferred to slink away and hide, or to never engage in the first place.

But just as she's about to explain these things yet again or to try, she is saved by goose liver. The foie gras arrives with small toasts and figs, and Helen rubs her hands together with delight. It is a gesture that she often makes before a delicious meal, one that Roberta can't stand. When Helen rubs her hands together, her cheeks tend to puff out and her eyes squint up; she looks like a clown. But Roberta would never point this out, because suffering through her sister's thirty-second lampoon of herself is much easier than hurting her feelings.

"Do you know how they make this stuff?" Helen asks. "They force-feed a goose, just force open its mouth and stuff cornmeal down it, until its liver doubles to twice its normal size. Then they kill it, and we get to eat the rewards."

"Sounds inhumane."

"It is," Helen says agreeably. "But foie gras is extremely delicious."

Roberta takes a bite; it turns out foie gras *is* extremely delicious, rich and smooth. Because Roberta likes animals little more than she likes her fellow human beings, she feels no guilt about savoring each small bite. Chewing, she fervently wishes she could eat real food, restaurant food, more often. This summer she's been living on cans of Del Monte corn and spinach salad—it's been too hot and she's been too cheap to buy or eat anything else.

"Mmmmm . . . " she says out loud, and Helen licks her fingers in agreement.

In June, Roberta visited her parents at their house on Cape Cod, and there she ate steamed clams and peach cobbler and corn from the cob instead of the can. She drove her mother's Range Rover to the beach and stuck her toes in the sand and thought idly about the novel she'd been writing on and off since college. Her parents had asked her about it, and she remarked that the plot was still "under construction," and she knew they thought she was a little bit shiftless but that didn't bother her. What business was it of theirs? Anyway, Helen was the one who cared about their parents' reactions. Helen was nine minutes older.

Roberta returned to the city as June ended. She paid her bills, went to the movies four nights in a row, and sat in Barnes and Noble each day reading *People Magazine* and *The New York Review of Books.* A week later the first heat wave of the summer started; Roberta woke up and found three gray hairs. The collusion of those two events seemed a signal to her to work on the novel, so she dug her six-year-old laptop computer out from under the futon, turned it on, and stared at it for a while. She ate a plum, dribbled juice onto the keyboard, and kept staring. "I am infinitely patient," she thought to herself. Finally, at four o'clock that afternoon, whatever muse she'd been waiting for struck, and she began to type.

At midnight, Helen called. "I'm at the office. You awake?"

"I'm writing!" Roberta said.

"I'm so proud of you!" Helen said, her voice full of cheer even though she had been wearing high heels for at least, Roberta estimated, fourteen hours. "You wanna go get drunk?"

"Sure!" Roberta said. So she met Helen and Richie down at the Big Bear Bar and Lounge and drank pitchers of Rolling Rock and staggered home at two in the morning, woozy in the late-night heat. That was a month ago, and she hadn't opened up the laptop since. The muse, she decided, must not like to hang out in apartments that don't have air conditioning.

"You're daydreaming," Helen accuses as the waiter replaces the foie gras plates with langoustine ravioli.

"Sorry," Roberta says. "I was just thinking about what a treat this is, to eat all this good food."

"You know," Helen says, "if you went out on dates, you'd get to eat in decent restaurants all the time." Oh God, Roberta thinks. Back to this.

"It's not worth it," Roberta says. "Dating, I mean. Who pays? Who calls? It's too confusing . . . "

"You always say that," Helen says. "But I've stopped buying it. Either you're afraid of something, or you're a lesbian, in which case I know this really pretty woman in contracts . . . "

"I'm not a lesbian," Roberta says. "I hate it when you start suggesting I'm a lesbian."

"Well, this dating phobia doesn't make any sense," Helen says, through a healthy bite of langoustine ravioli. She chews, swallows, cuts another piece. "And I worry about you. I want you to be happy. I mean, Roberta, you've got such a pretty face. You could conquer the world with such a pretty face."

"You don't have to worry about me," Roberta says, wondering if resentment is leaking through her voice.

"But I do, I do . . . " Helen is stuffing the langoustine down, really going at it, as though the food were going to save them both.

"I mean it, Helen. Don't worry about me. I'm happy."

"Look, just give the paralegal a call," Helen says, swallowing. "At the very least you'll probably get a free meal out of it."

"Are you listening to me at all?" Roberta says. "I'm not going to go out with a guy just for a free meal." She speaks in a steely tone that her sister does not hear.

"Why not?" Helen says blithely. "I would."

"Helen," says Roberta, "the last thing in the world you need is a free meal."

There is a beat, a whole note of silence. Roberta reviews what she has just said and feels heat rise from her jawbone up into the middles of her cheeks.

Twins are supposed to share an expanse of knowledge, a communal understanding and point of view. There is also, supposedly, the bizarre paranormal experience that occurs when one twin stubs her toe and the other one feels it. But Helen and Roberta have been denied these strange blessings of twindom because they don't look alike and never have. Helen's heft (or is it Roberta's relative slenderness?) prohibits them from sharing the sensation of what happens to the other's body. Instead, they have experienced the world as jolly versus quiet, lazy versus athletic, fat versus thin. Roberta has never known what it is like to be given extra room on an uncrowded train. She could not possibly imagine, nor has she ever really tried.

Helen's face is slowly returning to color, but Roberta knows that she herself is still red.

"I'm sorry," she says, softly. "Helen, I didn't mean anything by that, I don't know what I was saying, I'm sorry—"

"No, you're right," Helen says, and Roberta can see she's being careful with her words. "I don't need any free meals. I mean, I make over two hundred thousand dollars a year."

"Exactly," Roberta says and then takes a sip of wine. She takes another, wipes her mouth, and puts the wineglass back on the table. "That's exactly what I meant."

"No, it isn't," Helen says. "But I'll let it go."

Roberta nods. She turns her gaze down at her food. Automatically, mechanically, she begins slicing and eating, slicing and eating. It is only when she notices silence across the table that she stops and looks up again.

"You're not eating?"

"Well, you're right, I guess. That I probably should lose weight for the wedding photos," Helen says. She pokes at the food with a fork. "I shouldn't be stuffing my face."

"Don't be ridiculous," Roberta says. "You look beautiful, and it's our birthday, and this food is delicious. You should eat."

Helen sighs, pushing her plate away. "I'm not hungry . . ."

She covers her mouth with her hand for a moment, and Roberta is stricken with the immediate fear that her sister might throw up all over the food, her beaded blouse, the expensive-looking table linens.

"Oh, God," Roberta says. "I didn't say . . . I mean, don't—"

But then Helen moves her hand away and takes a sip of her water. "Water," she says. "No calories, very filling. The perfect food. If I could live on nothing but water . . ." She picks up her fork and trails it around her plate, streaking a circle in the red pepper coulis that surrounds her ravioli. "Then I'd be a skinny little butterfly myself."

"Helen, don't be—"

"Don't be what?" Helen asks, and now she is smiling. "Don't be what?" She dabs at her lips again with her spattered linen napkin. "Why don't you tell me about your novel?" she says.

"What?"

"The novel," Helen says, still patting at her mouth. "The big project. The goal, the objective. Your life's work." She drops the napkin in her lap. "How goes it?"

"Are you really not going to eat anymore?"

"I want to hear about your book." Helen's hands are now on the table, and her lips are pressed together in a tight, purposeful way. "Or have you given up again?"

Roberta cuts a piece of ravioli, looks at it, and doesn't pick it up. "I'm on chapter six," she says, flatly. "Will you please eat, Helen? It's our birthday."

"And what happens in chapter six?"

"I don't know," Roberta says. "It's not done yet."

"Well what happens in chapter five?"

"I forget," Roberta says. "It's not very good."

"Isn't it?" Helen asks, taking another sip of her water. "But you've been working on it for six years."

"On and off," Roberta says.

"Off and on," Helen says. The waiter appears to take away their plates, and looks questioningly at them both when he sees that several of their ravioli are still on their plates. "Take 'em," Helen says, waving her hand airily. "I'm full."

Roberta watches sadly as the waiter nods, bends, and carries away two plates of some of the most delicious food she's ever known.

"Are you really full?" she asks.

"I remember when you first told me about the novel a couple of years ago, back when you were deciding about graduate school. Remember?"

"I guess—"

"I was so impressed with you," Helen says, and takes another prim sip of water. "I mean, my sister the novelist, the master's degree in English, a real literary life, while I'm slaving away at the law for my own materialist ends."

"Helen, what are you getting at?"

"I mean, here's a woman who you can't count on to leave her apartment for a whole month, so who better to write a novel, right? Right?"

There is another beat of silence, after which Roberta says:

"I didn't mean to call you fat, Helen."

"Who mentioned fat, Roberta?"

They stare at each other as the waiter brings their monk-fish and stare at each other some minutes later, when he takes their still-full plates away.

The Manhattan night is now dark, but still hot, sticky, and slow. The sisters have not spoken much since Helen said, "No dessert, no coffee, just the check, thanks."

"Are we still meeting Richie?" Roberta asks cautiously, because fighting with her sister leaves a concave space in her gut, and she does not want to leave Helen's presence until they've reconciled.

"We were never meeting Richie," Helen says.

"What?"

Helen turns, and Roberta can see that sweat has already dampened her blouse. "We were never meeting Richie," she says again, and then lifts her arm to hail the first passing cab. Before Roberta can figure out whether or not to follow her sister in, Helen has closed the taxi door and driven off.

"Shit," Roberta says, watching the taxi disappear down Sixty-third. The heat wraps around her like a hug, and she feels herself begin to sweat underneath her bangs. "Shit," she says again, checking her wallet. She has a single dollar bill, which is not enough for a cab. It is not even enough for sub-way fare. About the only useful thing a dollar bill can get her is a cold Poland Spring from the market across the street. After making her purchase, she takes a deep breath, and then begins the slow, hot walk toward Gramercy.

A half hour later, Roberta stands in the marble-tiled hall

of Helen's building, knocking. Several minutes go by before her sister opens the door.

"You walked here?" Helen says. She has taken off her beaded blouse and now wears a Knicks T-shirt over her long cotton skirt.

Roberta, streaked with mascara and gummy with sweat, sags against the doorframe. "Can I come in?"

"Sure," Helen says, backing up. Her spare, bright apartment is air-conditioned to a frosty sixty-eight degrees. "I can't believe you walked here."

Roberta totters into the galley kitchen, which overlooks the spacious beige living room. She pours herself a glass of iced tea and drinks it while standing in front of the open refrigerator. When she has emptied her glass, she refills it and empties it again. Then she closes the refrigerator, puts the glass in the sink, and turns to face her sister. "What was that bullshit at dinner?"

"Excuse me?"

"We stopped talking halfway through dinner," Roberta says. "Didn't you notice?"

Helen lifts her shoulders and then drops them heavily, as if to indicate she doesn't know what Roberta's talking about. Then she walks into the living room, plants herself on a beige leather couch, and sighs. "Could you get me some iced tea?"

"No," Roberta says. She kicks off her sandals and can feel the stench of her own feet rise up and hit her. Helen smells it too; she grimaces and then smiles. Roberta grimaces and smiles back. "Are we going to talk about it?"

"Hmm . . . " Helen says. She examines her perfect pink fingernails for a moment, and then looks up. "Did you know Richie and I haven't had sex in weeks?" she asks. She leans back into the sofa and smiles a tempered smile. "It's true. I mean, sometimes we'll snuggle or something, but then—it fizzles. We don't talk about it."

"Why not?" Roberta asks warily.

"Not sure, really," Helen says. She examines her fingernails again. "I guess I'm afraid to hear his explanations. And when we first met, we did it all the time. Really. Like rabbits."

Roberta winces. She sits down on the loveseat opposite her sister but doesn't meet her eyes. "So what are you going to do?"

"Nothing," Helen says. "I've put on thirty pounds since I first met Richie. I know, it's a lot. Hard to tell, because I was fat to begin with, but even on me, thirty pounds is something . . . When Richie and I first met, he didn't care that I was plump. That was his word, *plump*. He thought I was beautiful and told me so and that was as happy as I ever thought I'd be. And so, you know, I started eating again, really letting myself eat, because I was so damn happy." Helen laughs, but Roberta's sweat will not evaporate in her sister's chilly living room; she feels herself grow clammy and cold and can't join in the laugh.

"Anyway, at first Richie wanted me to see a doctor. Said he was worried about my health. But then later he just stopped touching me, and I don't think he was worried about my health anymore. I just don't think he could bear it."

"Helen . . . "

"The saddest part is that I still love him," Helen says. She looks down at her hands now as she talks. "I love him. We've been together for three years, you know, and I know him about as well as I've ever known any man, and I think he's a good person and kind and all that. I mean, I respect him, I . . . " She looks up. "It saddens me to think that Richie doesn't want me anymore. It scares me to death that he'll say it out loud."

Roberta, who has never known heartbreak, can suddenly imagine how it feels.

"So this is why," Helen continues, "when I see you staying in your little steam room apartment, and you're not going out, and you won't pick up the phone—it kills, me, Roberta. If I had what you had . . . " Helen takes a gulp of air and pushes herself up off the loveseat, and Roberta can see those thirty extra pounds clinging to her sister's body like needy children. The Knicks T-shirt folds and curves around each bulge, the loose cotton skirt forms to each of her sister's blocky thighs. My sister's as big as the moon, Roberta thinks to herself. My sister is the big bright fat shining moon.

"I think I'm going to go to sleep," Helen says after a few moments. "I'm tired. You can stay here if you want."

"Are you still getting married?" Roberta asks quickly.

"I assume so," Helen says. "I'd like to. It's always been the main thing I've wanted."

Roberta looks up at her moon-faced sister and wishes with whatever energy she has left that she could take her back to the steps behind the porch, to the mosquitoes, to the Jack Daniels, to "Danke Schoen" and "Don't You Want Me,

Baby." But she can't. They will be here, in the air-conditioned apartment on Gramercy, until time pushes each of them forward in its own specific, moon-faced, heavy way. Roberta thinks to herself that she should probably get going.

"I'll tell you something else, though," says Helen, as Roberta stands up. "Being in love is fun. Or it can be. You should try it some time."

"It doesn't seem like too much fun," Roberta says.

"I know." Helen looks at her feet ruefully. "I wish I could have done a better job of convincing you. I always wanted to convince you—I didn't want you to end up alone. I didn't want either of us to end up alone."

Roberta takes another close look at Helen, who once again looks like her sister, who no longer resembles the moon. "Well, we have each other, right?" she says.

"We do," Helen says. "But we're older now, and it's not enough anymore."

When Roberta stumbles back out into the night, the heat seems to have broken a little. She can stand still for a moment without sweating. She turns around and looks up at her sister's tall brick building, with the elevator and the doorman. In her own apartment, there is the safety of chain locks and white walls and laundry baskets and fans. A laptop computer and, if she remembers correctly, a couple of beers in the fridge. But her own apartment is four miles away, and she still has no money.

"Happy birthday," she says to herself out loud, and then begins the slow walk north, toward everything she has.

Family Vacation

WE WENT TO DISNEY WORLD. Of course we did. I was just about to turn seventeen, graduating high school a year early, and there I was, on the Monorail with Aunt Minnie and Uncle Bill and Sally and Rita and Stu. Aunt Minnie, I know, like Minnie Mouse. Believe me, the coincidence was discussed hourly.

Oh, and Rita was my mother, and Stu was my father, and Sally was my retarded little sister—I mean, these relationships still hold, but in order to set the stage properly I'm going to put everything into past tense. And Sally really was a retard. Ten years old and she couldn't tie her shoes. Okay, I know, retard's not really the sensitive term, and these days everybody wants to be sensitive. So I guess if you want the real definition, Sally was a mildly autistic Down's syndrome child with severe food allergies and a piss-poor temper, who shit in her pants frequently and wasn't even cute in that gosh-I-feel-sorry-for-her-let's-donate-to-a-cause type of cute that retard kids sometimes are. To be honest, Sally wasn't even particularly nice, and she repeated everything she heard, which is why she wasn't allowed to watch TV.

But anyway—the Monorail, and all of us on it, in April. Minnie sat there, pregnant to the extreme and grimly worried that her baby would turn out "special," just like our Sally. Didn't mention it much, but it was written on her face. Plus it was her first baby, and she was thirty-nine, and she'd put on forty-two pounds with this pregnancy and thought for sure that weight gain was a Sign of Something. She was wearing a Minnie Mouse T-shirt, size obese, and smiling gamely, and Bill was clutching her hand with intensity. They gazed out onto the central Florida landscape beneath the Monorail. Sally sat opposite them, picking her nose.

My parents sat on the bench seat across from me. They did not hold hands, but this wasn't due to some sort of tacit hostility. My parents were relatively happy with each other, just tired. They were and always had been the sort of people who expected life to announce a fresh disaster any second, and this was an exhausting way to live. But they remained cheerful due to a God-fearing Christian spirit and the fact that, as far as they knew, I hadn't yet turned to drugs.

"This thing doesn't seem to be moving much, does it?" asked Uncle Bill, staring out the window. We were the only people in our Monorail car, but it still wasn't clear if he was talking to all of us or none of us.

A few minutes later, Minnie said, "No."

"I wonder if it's stuck," my father said.

"Stuck stuck stuck stuck stuck . . . " said Sally.

"That's right, hon," said my mother. "Stuck."

"Gee," Minnie said, thoughtful. "I hope not."

"Maybe the Monorail's broken. Maybe we'll be sitting here forever, waiting for the oxygen to run out. Maybe some of us will starve to death, and the survivors will have to feast on each other's remains like a latter-day Donner party," I said.

A second or two passed. "Maybe," my mother responded.

"Or those guys in the Andes."

"I really hope it's not broken." That was Minnie again. "I have to pee." Minnie's twin concerns during the past two days had been wondering whether or not Space Mountain would hurt the baby and finding public restrooms.

"Pee pee pee pee pee."

"Can you hold it, honey?"

"I guess so."

"Look out there," my dad said. "I think I can see an alligator. They don't have alligators in New Jersey."

"No," said my mother. "They don't."

We were silent. Then I said, "Except at the zoo," just to heighten the inanity.

"Yes," my mother said. "They have alligators at the zoo."

Well, like I said, I was turning seventeen in the imminent future and felt bad about wasting any more of my sixteenth year on the Monorail. But there we were, and the minutes passed, and then Goofy boomed out over the P.A. system like the voice of God.

"Hey there, folks," he said, in his supremely aw-shucks Goofy voice. "Sorry 'bout the inconvenience, but we're experiencing a few technical difficulties. Don't worry—huh-huh—we'll have you back on the road in a jiffy."

"You know, Minnie," I said, "if this were a sitcom, you'd be going into labor right about now."

"Erin," my mother warned.

"I'm not due for another month and a half," Minnie said primly.

"Does the baby know that?"

"Erin!"

"Sorry."

"I saw the doctor two days before we left. He said I was in perfect shape, that the baby wasn't moving anywhere for at least five weeks."

We paused, and I'm sure we were all considering the doctor's credibility. I mean, Minnie looked like she was ready to birth an elephant.

"Actually, we're thinking about inducing labor," said Bill after a while.

"Inducing labor?" I asked. "Why?"

"Well, that way we can plan the baby's birthday, be all ready to go. Packed up and everything. No late night surprises," he said and ran his hand through his thin blond hair.

"Aren't babies supposed to be surprising?" I asked. Nobody answered. So then, okay, I tossed out another question. "How do you induce labor?"

"You get this shot of hormones that bring on contrac-tions."

"Does it hurt?" I asked.

"Not at all," said Bill.

"Sally, stop it!" my mom yelled. Sally had evidently found something really interesting in the recesses of her nose and was smearing it across the shiny Disney Plexiglas. "Nice girls don't do that, Sally."

Sally looked at my mother with profound indifference.

"Come here, button," my father said to her, but Sally turned her same tuna fish gaze onto him. Her lips were pink and moist with saliva.

"I really do have to go to the bathroom," said Minnie. "I hope this starts soon."

"I remember that was the worst part of being pregnant," said my mother. "The absolute worst. I couldn't sleep, I could never sleep on my back, and then when I finally did fall asleep I had to get up and pee."

"All the time, she had to pee," said my father. "I'd never seen anything like it."

"And you didn't even put on half this much weight. Not with either of them."

"Well, that doesn't mean much, Minnie. Didn't the doc-tor say it was fine?"

"He told me not to eat so much ice cream."

"You wouldn't believe the way she's been eating ice cream," said Bill. He held Minnie's hand more tightly. I could see the white around his knuckles. "I've never seen anyone eat ice cream like that."

"What flavor?" I asked. "I heard vanilla's not so good for the developing fetus."

Minnie and Bill both turned to me, open-mouthed. "Must you say things like that?" asked my mother. "Must you?"

"Oh, please, Mom," I said. "It's like a right of adolescence." I paused for a groan of appreciation; got nothing but empty looks. "Get it, guys? Right of adolescence? Right, like it's my right, not R-I-T-E, like a synonym for ritual, you know? Adolescent rites?" Oh, screw it. "No pun intended," I muttered.

Bill replied, but too softly to hear.

"What was that?" I asked.

"Nothing."

"No, really. I want to know."

"Everything you do is intended, Erin. Everything." He let go of Minnie's hand and stood up. "It's getting hotter in here."

"What do you mean, everything I do is intended? Of course everything is intended. Is that a bad thing?"

"It's a right of adolescence," said Bill. Minnie sat there with her arms crossed on her belly.

"I don't get it. I really don't. What's so bad about being intentional? Didn't Thoreau wish to live deliberately?"

He was standing at the end of the Monorail. We were in the last car, and from the rear we could see a curve of white track stretched out like bone. "I went to the woods so that I could live deliberately," Bill said, and it sounded like he was making fun of me.

"Or something like that." I slumped back in my seat, trying to figure out Bill's problem. He had shown up in our lives two years before, saving Minnie from an impending forty-something full of pottery-throwing and cats. He was an accountant, balding, near fifty, divorced, and kidless. He had seemed kind and sort of witty. We used to trade wisecracks and make fun of each other, and he would bring me presents: interesting books and Haagen-Dazs. Of course, even at fourteen I knew that the best thing about Bill was that he loved Aunt Minnie despite her broad hips and her neediness. Everyone greeted him with such *relief*. Anyway, they got married a year later; he whisked her away to Boca Raton and bought her a Pontiac with a sunroof.

Shaking me out of what my mother would call a brood, merciful Goofy returned. "Hey there, folks. Sorry 'bout the inconvenience, but we're experiencing a few technical difficulties. Don't worry—huh-huh—we'll have you back on the road in a jiffy."

"I wish someone would let us know what's going on," my mother said. Sally was now sitting on her lap, sucking on her left hand.

"It's just like Goofy said. A few technical difficulties," said Bill. He had perched himself on the edge of a seat and was smiling tightly around his teeth.

"Goofy knows," I said.

"Goofy knows all," Bill agreed, and he loosened up his smile a little.

"I swear I might pee in my pants. We all just might float away," said Minnie.

"Hey there, folks ... " said the all-knowing Goofy and then was mysteriously quiet.

We all were silent then, following Goofy's lead. My sister made soft noises with her tongue as she sucked on my mother's hand.

I was six years old when Sally was born. I had prayed desperate prayers for a little sister, told God I'd give up my bicycle and my new soccer cleats for another girl in the house. Boys, I knew, were truly gross, even the ones I had crushes on; they wouldn't let me dress them up and they always wanted to cut worms in half instead of playing Barbie. A girl, I reasoned, would get a whole new set of Barbies that I could steal—and I could dress her up in my mom's old clothes and make her look like a movie star. Plus, Amanda Rigger told me that sisters (she had three, idiots all) were much stupider than brothers (she had one, at Harvard), and even back then there was nothing I liked more than being smarter than someone else.

My parents had been promising me a brother or sister for years, and then made me wait, and wait, and wait again. For instance, my fifth birthday: my parents woke me up, handed me several elaborately wrapped presents, and then told me that I'd get the best present of all in a few months. I didn't need them to spell it out for me—I jumped out of bed and ran around my room, spinning manic circles like some demented wind-up toy. "A new baby! A baby! A baby!"

I decided not to ask too many questions about the baby, for I was dimly scared that discussing the miracle might make it disappear. But the curiosity! The fantasies! And I guess like any little kid, I had no patience at all; when I couldn't stand it any longer I brought up the subject—hesitantly. My mother and I were driving home from soccer, and I asked her, in a small voice, what we might name the baby. She pulled over onto a side street and looked at me carefully. "The baby . . . well, this baby decided not to come home with us right now. It . . . the baby decided—the baby decided to go to heaven instead."

"Heaven?"

"Heaven . . . I know. I'm so sorry, honey." And I remember not being too surprised. I remember thinking I just *knew* something like this was going to happen.

Finally, I asked, "Why heaven?"

"Oh, Erin," said my mother, turning her attention back to the road, "I wish I knew."

It was only a year later, but it seemed like an infinity of waiting and hoping. My parents stole off to the hospital late one Saturday night. Aunt Minnie woke me up around nine the next morning.

"You have a sister," she said. She was smiling broadly.

I swallowed hard. I had suspected something was up. "When can I see her?"

"Soon."

Well, of course neither Minnie nor I knew I wouldn't meet my sister for another two months. There were complications; she was in and out of the intensive care unit, not responding properly to medicine or stimuli. She refused to feed, I found out later. My father came home briefly one Sunday night; he hugged me and then picked up the phone. He was talking to his mother, Grandma Sally. He said in the eerily resigned voice that would become the only voice he had that something was very wrong.

My mother came home a week after that. She told me that the baby's name was Sally, like Grandma, and that I would meet her soon. She said that the baby was very pretty, with big blue eyes but no hair. She also said that the baby was too small to come home but would become big and strong soon. The baby was very tired, she said. So was she.

Minnie stayed with us for a month, commuting into the city for work and doing all of the cooking, the cleaning, the laundry. My dad went to the office three days a week and to the hospital the other four. My mother visited the hospital when she could to see the baby, but most of the time she watched game shows or read. She took a lot of baths. Minnie drove me to school, to soccer, to gymnastics. She arranged play dates for me and corrected my homework. Sometimes my mom or dad would tuck me in, but usually Minnie did, and I remember feeling kind of guilty that I liked Minnie's tuck-ins better. Mom and dad didn't seem to have their hearts in it anymore.

And so, a conversation: "Hey, mom?"

"Yes?"

"When can I meet the baby? I really want to meet her. Everyone's gotten to meet the baby but me."

"I know, honey. But the baby's not big enough to meet you yet."

"But when Amanda Rigger's mom had a baby she brought her right home and we got to play with her like as soon as she got home."

"Well, Sally's a different kind of baby than Amanda Rigger's sister. She's a special baby."

I thought about this. "If she's so special why can't I meet her? I'd be really nice to her."

"Oh, Erin, I know you would." I remember she turned her head, let her blond hair fall in her eyes. "You'll meet her soon, honey. I promise." She went upstairs before I could ask any more questions, and Minnie brought me cookies.

But my parents have always been good about promises. A week later, they brought me to the hospital. The baby lay there, behind a glass window, in a clear plastic bassinet. There were tubes and a monitor that made a steady beeping noise. The baby's head was big, but the rest of her was tiny. She stared at me and didn't blink. I had never seen such a strange-looking baby—Amanda Rigger's sister had been so perfect and little and pink. And of course, Amanda had gotten a wireless model. Here was my sister, and not only did she have wires and tubes and monitors, but she had a head the size of a cantaloupe and the body of a rag doll. She was like a total space invader.

I made a face at the baby, just to see what would happen. Whenever we made scary faces at Amanda Rigger's sister, she would start to cry. But this baby just stared at me, as wide and gape-eyed as a tuna fish.

I knew then that the baby was broken.

"I'm not kidding when I tell you that if I don't pee soon there will be a catastrophe."

"Well, what do you want me to do, Minnie?"

"I'm not saying you have to do anything, Bill. I'm just venting a little."

"Well, there's nothing we can do."

"I'm not saying there's anything you can do. I'm just expressing my need to go to the bathroom."

"Which you've expressed five times in the past half hour."

"I didn't realize you were counting."

"Neither did I."

We were getting pretty sick of each other, I can tell you that. Goofy hadn't made any more metaphysical appearances or apologies, and I realized then that Disney vacations are so fabulous because really, when everything works right, you don't have to talk to your other traveling companions at all. I mean, typical Disney dialogue:

"Wow, look at that line."

"Yeah, that's some line."

Pause.

"Well, instead of waiting on line, let's eat a nutritionally suspect Disney lunch or else buy some adorable if overpriced Mickey Mouse paraphernalia at one of the three thousand Disney shops conveniently located all over scenic Disney World."

"Okay."

Pause.

"But doesn't that Pirates of the Caribbean sound neat? You know what? Let's wait on line."

However, when the system fails, and you're stuck in a Monorail for half an hour or eternity, whichever comes first, with five other people who don't have much to say to you

and to whom you have absolutely nothing to say, or at least nothing to say that won't get you smacked—well, that's when the Disney philosophy breaks right on down. Lawsuits have been won over less. I mean, Disney sticking you on a Monorail for a half an hour without animatronic figures, dancing people in bear costumes, a faux Eiffel Tower? Come on, man. That's like breach of contract.

And we were all getting testy.

"Listen, let's change the subject," said my mother. "Minnie, have you decided between Benjamin and Jonathan?"

"Oh, I don't know." Minnie adjusted herself laterally on the seat. "Benjamin Jonathan? Jonathan Benjamin? I'm sort of sick of both names, I've been thinking about it so much."

"And what if it's a girl?" my dad asked.

"I don't know," said Minnie. "I kind of like Valerie."

"Uch, no," I said, before I could stop myself.

"What's wrong with Valerie?" Bill asked. I could tell he wanted me to say something snotty. He wanted to yell at someone who wasn't Minnie.

"Oh, I don't know. There's a Valerie in my math class, and she's like a total idiot."

"That doesn't mean that all Valeries are total idiots," Bill pointed out.

"I know, but . . . "

"But what?"

"Well, I just don't want to have any negative associations with this baby. You know? Like if her name is Valerie, and I just meet her with all these bad Valerie connotations in my

head, then maybe my relationship with her will be permanently scarred."

"That's ridiculous," Bill said.

"I guess."

We were quiet again. Sally shifted her head on my mother's shoulder. My father pulled a brochure out of his knapsack and started reading.

"Did you know there's a Moroccan restaurant in Epcot?" he asked us. "I don't think I've ever—"

"I mean it," Bill interrupted. "That's really one of the most ridiculous things I've ever heard. You're going to have problems with my child because of her name, because there's some stupid girl in your math class . . . "

"That's not what I said. Forget it."

"That's exactly what you said. That's what you said, that you'll have negative associations with our daughter . . . "

"Bill, leave her alone," said Minnie.

"No, I just want to know what she means. She's been obnoxious all day, and I'd just like her to explain herself."

"Obnoxious?"

"Bill . . . " Minnie reached out to touch his arm, but he jerked away.

"I just don't know why everyone's so willing to put up with her crap. Vanilla ice cream is bad for the fetus? Valerie's a bad name? Why are we listening to this?"

"Bill, she's sixteen."

"Almost seventeen," I said.

Bill snorted and stood up again, walked to the rear window. I was more curious than angry. Sure I was obnoxious, I

knew it, but obnoxiousness had become my hallmark. I mean, I had been way more obnoxious when Bill first met me two years before, and he'd never seemed to mind. In fact, he had always seemed to get a kick out of it. What happened?

"Attention, passengers," a human voice announced. We all looked up toward the ceiling as if the voice issued from the heavens and not the public address system. "Excuse us for the delay. We are experiencing track difficulties, but we should be on our way again within fifteen minutes."

"The lines will be awful by the time we get there," said Minnie.

"Oh, it won't be so bad," my father said. "And we could have Moroccan food for dinner. That would be fun. It says here they have belly dancing."

"Belly dancing? In Orlando?"

"They also have a log flume ride through Norway."

"Because that's actually the traditional way to see Norway," I pointed out. "On a log flume."

"I didn't realize that Norway was located so close to Morocco," my mother reflected.

"It's the magic of Disney," I said.

My mother smiled and rubbed Sally's head.

"I've always wanted to go to Scandinavia," said Minnie. "A friend of mine from college, she was from Sweden. She invited me to visit and I never did, but I should have." She patted her stomach thoughtfully. "I wonder whatever happened to her. Her name was Anna, I remember, and she had dark hair, which I thought was very unusual for a Swede."

"Swedes can have dark hair," I said. "My friend Bertram, his dad's Swedish, and his hair's like black. Kind of handsome."

"Oh yes," said Minnie, "the Swedes are a handsome people."

"I think all those Nordic types are quite handsome," said my mother.

"You could be Nordic yourself," Minnie said.

"Me? No, too short." My mom tapped her cheek, considering. "Well, maybe. Wouldn't that be nice, to be Nordic?"

"Sally too," said my father.

"Sure, Sally too. Why not?"

"Why not?" Bill echoed. A motor noise started, and we all held our breaths, but then the noise vanished and we didn't even lurch.

"You know where I've always wanted to go?" asked my father. "Greece."

"Greece?" Mom said. "You never told me that."

"Yeah, Greece. I always had this idea that the Greek islands would be really nice. Don't you remember seeing those photos of Jackie Kennedy on that boat?" He nodded slightly at the useless memory. "And what's that drink they have there, that liquor?"

"Orzo?" Minnie suggested.

"Yeah, orzo—no, that's not right—what's orzo?"

"Orzo," I said, "is an Italian rice-shaped pasta."

"It is?" asked Minnie. "I thought it was that Greek drink."

"Ouzo," Bill said.

"Huh?"

"The drink—it's ouzo."

"Right," said my dad, rubbing his chin. "It is called ouzo."

"I know." Bill looked angry. "Ouzo."

"Have you ever been to Greece, Bill?" my mother asked in her kindest voice.

"Nope." He stood up, sat back down, looked at all of us accusingly. "Never been to Greece."

"Well, maybe there's an Epcot Greece," Minnie mused. "It could have like a mini Parthenon and maybe some swarthy types serving orzo. I mean ouzo."

"Epcot Greece," Bill said roughly. He stood up and jammed his hands into his pockets; you could see his fists balled up underneath the fabric of his Dockers.

Okay, so Bill was angry. I was sure he was angry, but I also had no idea what to do about it. What could any of us do about it? None of us knew him that well, I guess; we had all been so eager to welcome him to the family that we didn't really consider the idea that he might be psycho. Then again, he had never come off as damaged, and it's not like we just shipped Minnie off to the first available customer. They dated, she introduced us, we approved—especially me. I mean, because let's face it: she loved him. She did. Even now, when he was shifting into weirdo mode, she still looked at him with all the gawpy idolatry of a basset hound.

"Bill, honey," she said, struggling to get to her feet, "what's the matter?" She stood up, balanced herself on a stainless steel support pole, and made sure her T-shirt fully covered her expanse of belly. "What's wrong?"

Three years ago, Minnie had been a low-level administrator at a technical company in the city; she had taken two pottery classes a week and studied yoga. She had two cats, both of whom she named after favorite writers (Ellison and Krantz). She had lived in a studio in the Village decorated with clay and Mostly Mozart posters. She went to jazz clubs sometimes. She took me to Serendipity for frozen hot chocolates and peanut butter sundaes. She'd had friends.

I had no idea what her life was like in Boca Raton; for some reason we'd all been sort of embarrassed to ask. She didn't work, I knew that. She read newspapers and decorated their spacious three-bedroom. She called us precisely two times a week and had suggested this vacation as a last hurrah for all of us—a chance to spend some quality time before The New Arrival, for the old team to bond before I headed off to college in the fall. Somewhere, I suspect, each of us knew there'd be a cataclysm—it seemed almost built into these kinds of vacations. The viciously enforced cheerfulness of a Disney escape seemed to include, by necessity, a brief moment of personal hell. This wasn't my personal hell, though. And my parents, looking comfortingly at each other and at Sally—well, their hells were behind them, I think. But Minnie looked scared.

"Bill," she started, holding tight to the pole. "Bill . . . "

"Nothing's the matter."

"Bill—"

"I said, nothing's wrong."

Oh sure, right. Bill was sitting, barely balanced at the edge of his seat. His sharp little elbows were pressing down on his knees, and his blond bony head was cradled in his fists.

"Well . . . " Minnie said, and looked pleadingly at the rest of us. When her eyes met mine, I looked down.

"Minnie, why don't you sit," said my father.

"I don't think I can—"

"Sit down, Minnie. It's all right," my mother soothed. Sally had transferred; she was now sucking vigilantly on my mother's right thumb.

"But I don't think Bill—"

Bill looked up. His eyes were slightly red, slightly narrower than they had seemed a few minutes before. His knuckles had made imprints at his temples, bright white on his rosy, vein-lined skin. "Minnie, sit."

"Please tell me what's wrong."

"Sit down."

"Please tell me." There was a shivering in her voice. I found it pathetic but also grossly embarrassing, and I realized suddenly that I was too old for family vacations.

Anyway Minnie, ever the make-peace, eased herself back down on one of the Monorail cushions. Her T-shirt rose slightly on her stomach, and we were treated to an uncomfortable view of her puffed-out belly button emerging like a bottle cap from her round, wide middle. Her face was collapsing. She adjusted her shirt.

"I wish you would talk to me, Bill."

"Talk?"

"I wish you would . . . "

My father was studiously reading his brochure. I stared at Sally, at my mother's hand moving over her blond wisps. Sally's eyes were closed, and she breathed in and out in a sleep-sloppy way. She had stopped sucking on my mother's thumb, but she held it in place in her mouth with her little chicken teeth. For the first time in my life, I wanted to be my sister.

"Bill?"

"What do you want from me, Minnie? What the fuck do you want from me?"

I closed my eyes.

"What the hell is it that you want me to tell you? We're in fucking Disney World with this family—with this freak of nature, we're here with the bitchiest sixteen-year-old I've ever met and this—this girl, this child, what is she? What is this? An idiot! We're here with this idiot, this, this freak, this is your family! What the hell do you want me to tell you?"

Nobody breathed, except for Bill, whose breath jerked out in sharp, jagged pants. I kept my eyes closed.

"This fucking idiot. What do you call her? Mongoloid?"

Pause.

"It's called Down's syndrome, Bill." I opened my eyes, and was surprised to see my mother still sitting there, still rubbing the head of sleeping Sally. "Our daughter has Down's syndrome."

Sally had completely passed out on my mother's lap, but she kept on sucking away, and my mother stuck a hand down her pants to see whether or not she was dry. Sally still wore diapers a lot of the time, but she had been refusing them lately, and so my parents had been experimenting with underpants. The day before we'd had to buy a whole new set of Indiana Jones panties and sweats in Adventureland. To make up for any perceived inequities, my parents bought me a jaunty Harrison Ford leatherette hat with a real rawhide strap. I wore it for about two minutes before I started to feel like a complete asshole.

Sally didn't like strangers, but she wasn't scared of them like some autistic kids. In fact, sometimes she approached strangers and did amusingly inappropriate things. Like for instance, after we bought her the Indiana Jones stuff, she decided that she was an action-adventure heroine out to save all of Disney World from some evil threat. She dashed in and out of lines, roaring and making faces at other tourists, at animals, at plasticized Disney employees masquerading as Pinocchio or one of the seven dwarfs. I put my hat on her head, and with her soft blond hair and huge blue eyes she was almost cute. The other people on line prodded each other, smiled their approval. "Look at that sweet little girl," they seemed to be saying with every nod. And okay, I know this sounds asinine, but honestly, I was almost proud of her. Like, yeah, isn't she cute?

"Roar, Erin," she said, running around me in circles as we walked toward Thunder Mountain Railroad.

"Roar, Sally," I replied. She threw my hat on the ground and starting jumping up and down with glee.

"Roar! Roarrrrrrr! Roar roar roar!" She bit my leg, but not hard, and then laughed so hard that tears started rolling down her cheeks.

"Yeah, Sally. Roar."

"Hahhhhhhh! Ha!" And she took my hand, which she had done maybe twice before in her life, and started run-

ning. And I ran with her, laughing and roaring, into the fat
sheep crowds of Disney.

Goofy broke the silence. "Hey there, folks. Sorry 'bout the
inconvenience, but we're experiencing a few technical difficulties. Don't worry—huh-huh—we'll have you back on
the road in a jiffy."

"I'm sorry," Bill whispered.

My dad and I looked at each other. I don't think either
one of us could have looked at him. We couldn't acknowl-
edge it, any of it.

"It's been so . . . it's just been . . . "

"I know, Bill," my mother said, but her face was resistant
and her voice was unkind.

"Aah . . . " He stood up again, paced. "When we get off
this thing, I think I'll . . . I think maybe it would be best if
I—maybe if I went home a little early."

"You don't have to leave, Bill," I said.

"No, no . . . I think I better . . . "

The motor noise started; the whole Monorail hummed, but
we didn't move. Minnie whimpered. "I just wanted a vacation,"
she said. "I just thought it would be nice if we all . . . "

The humming got louder. "I think we're finally going to
move," I said.

"About time," said my dad. He smiled at me, cautiously. I
smiled back to say that yes, I'd be fine, Bill couldn't hurt me.
He couldn't, you know.

Bill was sitting again, opposite Minnie, looking hard out
the window. I doubt he saw much.

We all waited to move.

"Hi hi hi hi hi hi . . . " Sally was up, she was rubbing her eyes and smiling. "Hi hi hi hi hi . . . "

"Hello, honey," said my mother. "Good morning!"

"Morning! Good morning!" Sally laughed. She was usually at her best right after a nap. "Good good!"

"Oh," said Minnie. I looked at her for the first time in what seemed like hours. Her face was red and wet; tears had left crooked tracks down her cheeks, and she looked like a fat little girl. Then I looked down and saw a large dark stain slowly spreading from between her thighs.

"I think I wet myself," Minnie said.

The Monorail moved forward, just a bit at first. Then it kept going.

"Well, that's okay, honey," my mother said. "Do you feel better?"

"Yes," Minnie said, faintly. "I do." She looked at all of us, blinked, rubbed her eyes. "I feel better now," she said.

I nodded at Minnie; I gave her what I could. She looked back at me shyly. She said, "I needed this," and wiped a hand across her face. I looked at my sister, and then out the window, and we all moved together toward Disney's promised land.

How the Stars Live

SHE DRAGS HERSELF into the hotel room clutching a duffel bag in both arms like it's a puffy blue baby. Her hair is short and flat against her skull; she's wearing her glasses, and she seems thinner. I haven't seen her in three weeks and flatter myself for a moment that it's been my absence in her life that has made her look like shit.

"Here are the rules," she says, dumping the duffel on the bed. She doesn't kiss me or smile. "Yes to weed, no to cocaine."

"Sure," I say. I sit down on the bed next to her duffel bag and watch her shake out her hair in the mirror. Her back is to me.

"Yes to fucking, no to I-love-you's."

I think to myself, when do we ever say I love you? She cracks her neck and shakes out her shoulders. I pat the space on the bed next to me. Yes to fucking.

She sighs, turns around, balances her long thin hands on her blue-jeaned hips. "Yes to food, yes to sleep," she says. "Jesus, I'm tired."

Emily's red-eye from New York to L.A. wasn't really a red-eye; due to the clock shift it's only two in the morning here, although for Emily it feels like five a.m. and she's been on two planes since yesterday evening. She'd flown through Vegas, and I imagined her there, smoking furiously, pulling down the handles of the airport slot machines again and again with a knotted stomach and a dwindling supply of quarters.

"What do you want to eat?" I ask.

"What do people eat in L.A.?" She finally sits down next to me on the bed and then falls backwards with a dramatic sigh, her white T-shirt rising so I can see her concave stomach. I bend down to kiss her belly button. "Food first," she says. "I'm hungry. A burger from room service."

"Of course," I say, reaching over her to pick up the phone.

"And some fries," she says. "And a Budweiser beer, or any other beer. And an ashtray. Are there any ashtrays in this room? Or is it true what they say about smoking in California?"

"It's true," I say, on hold for room service. "I had to clip the smoke detector. There's an ashtray in the bathroom."

Emily rolls over and pulls a pack of Marlboros from the outer pocket of her duffel. "Fucking California," she says.

Room service picks up, and I begin the dialogue: Perrier water, grilled calamari, burgers. I know Emily. "Hey, tough girl," I say. "You want medium rare?"

"Of course," she says.

"They do salad instead of fries."

"I want fries," she says, lighting her cigarette with a lighter I bought her last year, a bright red novelty shaped like a pair of lips.

"She wants fries," I tell the guy down in room service, and I can hear him tsk tsk.

"And the beer!" Emily calls out.

"And four Buds," I say, and hang up before the room service guy can tsk again. I go into the bathroom and bring Emily back an ashtray. She sits it down in her lap, and I take her feet in my hands and untie her sneakers for her, sitting on the edge of the bed.

"It was a long flight," she says. She closes her eyes. I drop her sneakers on the floor and pull off her socks, one at a time, slowly. "A long flight. And I took some melatonin, but it really didn't work—herbal medications are bullshit."

"We knew that," I say. I put my thumb on the ball of her left foot, and circle slowly, with increasing pressure. Emily leans back on the pillow and lays the ashtray on her pelvis. She reaches down across her body to ash her cigarette. I move the pressure of my fingers up and down her foot, circling.

"And there was this kid behind me, not a baby, a baby would have slept—this kid was like eight years old and just fucking yammered the whole time, airplane facts."

"Airplane facts?"

"Like the reason an airplane flies is because the curvature of the wing—" here she yawns—"the curvature of the wing causes the air pressure under the wing, in motion"—another yawn—"to exceed the air pressure over it. So the plane rises. And flies."

"The kid said this?"

"Yup." Her long arm, covered with fine dark hairs and ending in a row of brittle bitten nails, extends back down toward the ashtray. "And that there has never been a crash on a New York to Las Vegas route. Not since commercial airlines starting making Vegas a standard destination. In nineteen sixty-two, according to this kid."

"How was Vegas?"

She exhales. "I played airport slots. I lost fourteen bucks."

"In quarters?"

"In quarters." She stubs out the cigarette on her pelvis and her hipbone shakes. I move to her right foot, starting again at the ball, a hard pressure in the middle, circling. Her feet, like her hands, are long and dry. For a second I think about jerking her foot hard to the left, so that I can hear all those little bones snap.

"Las Vegas is the fastest growing metropolitan area in the country," she says. "Faster than Orlando. Faster than Phoenix."

"I had no idea Phoenix was a fast-growing metropolitan area." Up and down her foot. Up and down, slowly, toward her heel.

"You're underinformed, Russell," she says.

"Las Vegas, huh?"

"People like to gamble." She sits up and takes off her glasses. She rests them on the nightstand, and then puts her face up close to mine, her eyes narrow and blue. Her breath is stale. "Where's my food?" she asks. "I'm hungry."

I lean in and kiss her through her stale breath and her hard eyes. By the time room service comes, she's fast asleep.

I've been in L.A. for three weeks already, taking pictures for our annual "How the Stars Live" issue. Our "How the Stars Live" issue isn't that different from any other issue, except we get some tours of celebrity houses and take pictures of them with their kids. Today I'm going to see Clint Eastwood's daughter's house. Clint Eastwood's daughter, a blond named Allison, has had a few supporting roles in a few forgettable movies, but she lives in a terra cotta-tiled villa in Silverlake and her P.R. people are anxious for us to see her being natural, at home. Clint Eastwood's daughter has fantastic P.R. people, the best. They use me like a hammer.

Since I arrived in L.A. I've been living at the Santa Monica Pacific Shore Hotel and driving a Metro. I thought the Metro would win me points with Accounting because it's an economy car, light and cheap. Avis does these deals where you can rent a Geo for a month and they'll kick in a free extra week. Since I'm going to be in L.A. for five weeks total, I thought this Avis package was the way to go. Turns out I was wrong. A Metro is the worst possible machine to drive in L.A. It's worse than a Buick Skylark, worse even than an Olds Eighty-Eight. Maybe a Metro is the right kind of ride for Chicago or Boston, towns where you get in the car to go somewhere else. In L.A., you get in a car to live. I'm living wrong out here. But I didn't know.

Julia, my girlfriend, came out to visit two weeks ago, right after I got here. She looked at the Metro. "You'll regret it," she said. "Trade it in for an old Malibu or something, something real."

I'd actually been thinking the same thing, but once Julia suggested the trade, I got defensive. "This car gets great gas mileage," I said. "I can park it anywhere."

Julia sighed. "The magazine is paying for your gas, Russ," she said. "You're on a business trip. Stop being so damn responsible."

While Emily sleeps, her head pressed up against the wood-veneer headboard, I roll a small joint and watch her. She's not even in the sheets. Just stretched out across the blue nylon comforter in her jeans, using up the whole length of the bed. I want to take off her jeans while she sleeps. I want to crawl in there next to her. But if I do this, I know she'll wake up and be annoyed. She wants to sleep—I should let her sleep. I take a big pull on the joint, sit back, and wait for the weed to calm me down.

It's been two years now, on and off, that I've been watching Emily sleep. I started in the spring of 1999, when she spent four months being my girlfriend. Back then she lived on Orchard Street on the Lower East Side with a parakeet named Theo, who learned my name the first night I stayed there and shouted it throughout the night: "Oh Russell! Oh Russell! Oh Russell!"

The things Emily and I did back when we were dating— they were small things, easy things. We'd go to Jackson Heights for Pakistani food or Crown Heights for Jamaican. We hit all the church book sales, and walked home under the weight of twenty pounds of hardcovers in paper grocery bags. Once we went up to Bear Mountain and attempted to hike, but the muddy trails and fresh air made us nervous, and then Emily realized she forgot to bring cigarettes. We turned around, spent the rest of that afternoon in a bar in Harriman, drinking Michelob Lights and watching the Knicks play televised basketball.

It was good; all of that was good. But nevertheless, after a few months, I lost the control I'd always been so proud of, at least as far as women go. I lost the restraint. I started wanting Emily to need me more than she did, wanted her to call all the time, wanted her to spend more nights with me in Brooklyn than she did by herself on Orchard. All this wanting made me hate myself. So I stopped calling every day, stopped leaving messages on the machine for her and the parakeet.

And then she stopped calling every day.

I stopped fucking her at night.

She stopped kissing me good morning.

And after only a few short weeks of this kind of present-disappearing act, she lost patience. "Russell," she said to me one April night. We had just seen a revivial of *Love in the Afternoon*, which had this warm, romantic ending and encouraged in me a reminder of my affections toward Emily. "We don't have to do this anymore."

I took my hand out of hers. "That's it?" I asked.

"If you want to stop seeing each other, it's fine," she said. I tried to look at her face for some indication as to whether or not this was a bluff, but she just stared at my collar and kept her hands at her sides.

"You sure?" I asked.

"Sure," she said. Her voice was as flat as the street.

"Well then," I said. She looked up at me, her narrow eyes shining behind glasses. "I guess that's it," I said. I was slightly baffled, to be honest—that all this destruction had happened so silently.

"Don't look like that," she said. "You were going to do this anyway. I just beat you to it."

"I guess," I said. I tried to arrange my face to give a projection of nonchalance. "I guess I was. But probably not tonight."

"But soon," Emily said. "And I didn't have time to wait around." Then she leaned in and kissed me on the cheek, and then turned around quickly, walking south, down toward the Lower East Side.

I stood still on the corner, watching her tall thin shape vanish down the sidewalk. Why did I blink? Why hadn't there been some fighting? I sat down on the nearest stoop, lit a Camel, and tried to determine. She had just left me, like a breeze or a snatch of music or a squirrel.

And she didn't call. I expected her to, in my shitty apartment in Carroll Gardens, staring out the window, getting high. Women mostly call after situations like that, I've found—not necessarily to say that they've made a mistake, but maybe to get some closure or to tell you what an asshole you really are. When I stared out the window, high as a cloud, I became philosophical, if not any smarter. I thought: she didn't care enough to stop it, I didn't know how to keep it going, and then somehow we drifted. It happens like that.

Even if people don't grow apart, they don't necessarily grow together. If I'd had any pictures of Emily, I would have looked at them, searched for a clue in her sharp nose or the way she posed with her arms around me. But here I am, a fucking photographer, and I didn't have any pictures.

She didn't call.

And by the time she did call, I'd met Julia, and things were different. But I still don't think I was any smarter.

In the morning I wake up with a thick taste in my mouth and Emily's head cutting off the circulation in my arm. She twitches when she sleeps, like she's being subjected to a series of small shocks. I try to move my arm out from under her head. She twitches and rolls over. I go to the armchair in the corner, light a cigarette, and watch her.

My appointment's at three o'clock—I'm meeting Allison Eastwood and her manager at the Coffee Bean and Tea Leaf, and then we're going to walk her dogs, and then we're going to get a tour of the house. The we is me and the reporter, Mack, who sleeps with some of the actresses he does stories on. Mack's been encouraging me to party with him, meet some of his lady friends—he says he's sure I'd like what I'd find. All I need, Mack tells me, is a better car. But the truth is, with Julia in New York and Emily here, I don't need much more in the way of female attention. I'm having a tough enough time managing what I've got. Not that Mack's the kind of guy who'd understand.

In her sleep, Emily can sense that I'm watching her. She opens one eye. "Morning," she croaks.

"Morning, sweetheart."

"What time is it?"

I look across the room toward the clock radio. "Nine thirty," I say.

"Twelve thirty New York time," she says.

"You slept late."

She rolls over, and her small white breasts point up toward the ceiling. Julia has enormous breasts, almost vulgar, with eggplant colored nipples the diameter of coffee cups. Emily's breasts, once I got to know them again, started to strike me as sweet, where once I thought they were stingy.

I crush my cigarette out in the ashtray and get into bed next to her. I kiss her neck.

"My breath," she says.

"Who cares?" I say. I keep kissing her neck, put my hand on her shoulder, force her to stay where she is.

"I smell terrible," she says.

"Like roses," I say. I move my mouth up her neck to her ear, to the space behind her ear and in front of her hairline that, when properly licked, makes her moan. I lick properly.

"Ohmmm," Emily says.

When we were dating, we fucked, sure, but I don't remember it being much better than normal. Which is not to say it was worse. But it was what it was, comfortable, fine, and I could wake up in the morning and see her small breasts and not be overcome with the need to lick her hairline. But now—I'm not sure how she's done it, but I couldn't sleep the past few days, knowing she was on her way, knowing I'd have her to myself for three whole days without Julia or anyone else.

I'd wake up at five in the morning, go to my window, and stare out at the long gray Pacific, imagining the enormous amount of fucking that was to take place. With Emily. My own.

When we're done, she rolls over on top of me and kisses me extravagantly. Like roses.

She tells me she wants to eat breakfast out on the beach. I've tried to explain to her that L.A. isn't New York, you can't just hit a bodega and come back with a bag full of bagels and paper-cup coffee. It's hard to find take-out breakfast. "But they must eat breakfast here," she says. She's showered, smiling, wearing a long black skirt and a black cardigan and hoop earrings. She looks about as southern California as a pine tree, but I don't think she's going to care.

"They eat breakfast in hotels," I explain. "At about eight in the morning. I've been on six breakfast interviews since I got here."

"At eight in the morning?"

"Once at seven."

"Poor baby." She sits cross-legged on the bed, her choppy hair drying out in the central heat. February in L.A., sixty-eight degrees, management's got the central heating going like we're in Tahoe. I grab my rental keys off the wood-veneer dresser.

"You stay here," I say. "I'll forage."

"You're taking the car?"

"I'm telling you, sweetie," I say. "Nobody walks in this town."

She sighs, shakes her head, lies down on the bed, a long black shroud. "I'm going to take a nap," she says, and it's all I can do to keep my keys in my hand and not just jump back on top of her. I'm a goddamn teenager again around Emily.

"I'll be here," she says, which I think means she wants me to leave.

"I'll be back," I say, and head out into the thin air of the fourteenth floor of the Pacific Shore Hotel.

An hour later, we're on the beach and it's cold. Sixty-eight degrees sounds nice for a New Yorker's February, sounds like a wet dream, actually, and you'd think if you had the chance to be on a beach in that kind of February weather you'd strip down to your boxers and dive right in. In New York, I've walked along the Hudson in the winter and actually imagined diving in to it, so desperate I've been for water and the activities of summer. But in California, sixty-eight degrees is indoor weather. Anyway, Californians never swim in the ocean, because years ago God invented the pool.

Emily has filched the top sheet from our hotel room and pinned it down to the sand with our shoes. We sit leaning back on our hands and stare out at the ocean. "What's for breakfast?" she asks me.

"Oh, right, breakfast." I pull oranges, grapefruits, and strawberries from a white plastic grocery bag.

"Coffee?"

"They only had cappuccino," I say, pulling out two cardboard cups. "I got yours skim."

She nods and pulls a big box out of the bag. "And cornflakes."

"Organic cornflakes," I say. "Very delicious."

"Your brain's been addled." She rips open the box of corn-flakes and takes out a handful, munching on it as a breeze blows her hair straight up. I peel an orange and hand her a section. "Vitamin C," she says. "Thanks."

We eat like this for a while, noisily, with our hands, slurping our cappuccino out from under hard plastic lids. The sky is a thin blue and the wind is calm, and a few shorebirds stand near our sheet, waiting for dropped cereal or a shred of orange peel.

"Scavengers," Emily says, tossing the birds a few corn-flakes. "They'll take anything they can get."

I throw the scavengers a strawberry and they descend on it with a flutter of shrieks and wings. "What do you want to do today?" I ask.

"Sit out on the beach," Emily says, without considering. "Maybe booze it up this afternoon, have some sex tonight."

"That's it?" I ask. "You've never been here before. Isn't there anything you want to see?"

"Hmm . . . " she says. She digs in her bag for a cigarette, lights it with her hand cupped around to protect the flame. "Maybe I should see how the stars live," she says. She knows the theme of our celebrity issue.

"Oh, please," I say. "Believe me, it's no fun. You'd be better off checking out the Getty or Venice Beach or something."

"No," Emily says, stretching out on her back. She blows smoke up toward the sky, where it drifts off behind us, and I worry for a moment that smoking on the beach is illegal in California. "I have no interest in the Getty. Nor in Venice Beach. But it would be nice," she inhales, "to see how the stars live for real. Do they laze around on beach chairs all day? Have servants deliver them rice cakes and wine?"

"Rice cakes and wine?"

"Do they snap their fingers for manicures, pedicures, hot oil massages?"

"You wanna get a massage?"

"I'm just thinking . . . " Emily closes her eyes, takes a deep drag of her cigarette. "If I were a star, how would I get things done? What would I want? I mean, it's an interesting question. How the stars live. How I would live if I were a star."

"Would it be that much different from what you've got now?" I ask. "I mean, Em, there's nothing in the world that you really want that you can't get."

Emily cocks an eyebrow at me with her eyes still closed. "Manolo Blahnik sandals," she says.

"Well, within reason . . . "

"Trips to Paris," she says. "Harry Winston jewels. Dinner at Restaurant Daniel five nights a week."

"You wouldn't want to eat there five nights a week."

Emily opens her eyes, watches her smoke fade up and away. "Well, there are other things too," she says, her voice a little softer.

"What other things?" I ask.

I wait for a reply, but she doesn't say anything, just inhales on the Marlboro, exhales, ashes into the air. I don't push it. After a few minutes, she sits up, leans over, and drowns her cigarette in the sand near our sheet. "Oh, forget it, Russell," she says. "Who needs stardom, right? We have each other."

"Sure," I say, and kiss her on the neck, because once again, she's left me lost.

We don't go back to the hotel room until almost one, when I have to get dressed and prepare myself for the potential hour's worth of traffic separating me from Allison Eastwood. I invite Emily to come along.

"No way," she says. "I'm going to watch cable television and order room service. I'm on vacation."

"Are you sure?"

Her shoes are already off, and she's positioned herself on the bed, lying on her stomach, feet crossed in the air behind her. "What've we got here?" she asks. "HBO, HBO Plus, Cinemax . . . Ooh, look, the Playboy Channel! Forget it, sport," she says. "I'm here all day."

"Okay," I say. "But I don't want you bitching later that you were bored."

Emily turns her head to me, smirking. "When do I ever bitch about being bored?"

I shrug. She doesn't. That's Julia.

I come over to the bed to kiss her good-bye, and I can see she wants me to leave again, that while I'm kissing her she's keeping one eye trained to the HBO. I guess I can understand this. In Emily's boxy one-bedroom on Orchard Street, she has neither room service nor a king-sized bed nor— come to think of it—a television. Let the woman relax, I think. Get out of there.

But I can't. I put both my hands on her cheeks, force her attention on me as I kiss her.

"Okay," she says, biting my lip, laughing. "Leave," she says. "I wanna watch TV."

"Aren't you sorry to see me go?" I ask, dropping my camera bag on the bed.

"Aren't you coming back?" she asks me, still smiling.

"I just don't like leaving you alone here."

"What are you afraid of?" she asks. She picks up the remote control and fingers it with one ragged nail.

I don't know what I'm afraid of. Maybe that she'll pack up her bags and vanish. Maybe that reporter Mack will come by to pick something up and end up stealing Emily away. Maybe I'm afraid she'll realize that she still doesn't need me. I put my hands in my pockets and helplessly watch her change the channel.

"Okay," I say. "Good-bye."

The phone rings.

"Good-bye," she says. "Pick up the phone."

"I don't want to," I say.

"It could be your girlfriend," she says.

"I don't want to," I say again.

She turns off the TV. "Pick up the phone, Russell," she says. There's a new and different quality in her voice. The phone rings once more, twice, and then stops. In a moment, the red voice-mail button starts to blink. Emily and I both watch it.

Suddenly she's off the bed, digging through her bag for her cigarettes, her arm motions jerky, her head bent down.

"Emily?" I ask. "Em?"

"It's okay if you pick up the phone," she says, tossing shit out of her bag in search of the cigarettes. A cellphone, a lip-

stick, her red-lips lighter all end up on the floor. "I know you
live with her, Russell. You're not fooling me or anything by
not picking up the phone. If she's calling, talk to her. You
fucking *live with her*," she says again. "She has the right to
call you."

"Emily?"

She finally finds her cigarettes, sticks one in her mouth,
leans over and picks up the red-lips lighter. I keep my hands
in my pockets, watches as she lights up. "Either pick up the
phone when she calls or go out and do your camera thing, do
whatever it is you have to do, but I'm here on four precious
vacation days, so please don't ruin them. Just *go*," she says.
Her hands are shaking.

"Emily," I say. "I don't want to leave you alone."

"You left me months ago," she says. "I'm not even sure
what the fuck I'm doing here."

"Excuse me?" I ask.

"You left me months ago," she says again, and by the way
her chin points up toward the ceiling and her eyes get shiny
and narrow, I can tell that she means what she's saying. She
means it, but she's wrong. I never left her. She's the one who
walked down Eleventh Street. She's the one who never
called. She's the one I bumped into at a press party nine
months later and had to follow home at a distance, in a separate cab, and call up to her second floor window like a low-
budget Romeo and beg her to let me in. She's the one who
kicked me out two hours later. She's the one who doesn't
always return my calls. She's the one who almost didn't come
to California, until I offered to buy her a ticket—business

class, round trip. She's the one who doesn't need me. I know it, I'm sure. If she'd needed me, I never would have let her go.

"Emily," I say. "Please stop shaking."

"Never in my life," she says, sitting down at the edge of the armchair, "did I intend to be the other woman. It's no fun, Russell. It's not how the stars live."

"You've never even asked me to leave her," I say.

"I've never presumed that you would."

Behind Emily, beyond the window, is the long gray Pacific. It is dull and smooth, like a sheet of steel, but if I followed a line stretching across the water, it would take me to Hawaii, maybe Japan, and then on to India, Russia, different continents. Then the Atlantic. And then back to New York, the long way. Maybe to Eleventh Street. Maybe to the last place I stood where Emily still belonged to me. Maybe if I took that trip, I'd come back a little smarter.

"I didn't know," I say.

"No to apologies," Emily says, her eyes still narrow. "No to I-love-you's." She straightens her shoulders, blows a stream of smoke out her lips, and stares at me as if daring me to say it anyway.

"But I . . . " I start—and then don't finish, because I'm still doing what she tells me. She's long and tough, dressed in black, sucking down her Marlboro like it's providing nutrition. She's the best thing I've got. But I'm not going to apologize, and I'm not going to tell her I love her, because she says she doesn't want to hear it. So I guess she doesn't want to hear it. And all I want to do right now, all I've ever wanted to do, is to give Emily what she wants.

Gazelles

THERE'S A RUMOR going around that I gave blowjobs to the entire boys' soccer team behind the A&P. I have no idea how this rumor got started, since most members of the boys' soccer team wouldn't even pass a fart in my direction, much less hang out with me publicly. But, like a fever, the rumor has festered and gained momentum, and now I can barely walk down the hall without getting tripped, whistled at, or shunned. This is hard.

If my two years at Hills Regional have taught me anything, it's that high school is not for the weak. And unfortunately for me, at Hills Regional I am among the weakest. If high school were a nature special, I wouldn't even be the gazelle that spends the whole show fleeing the lions. I'd be the pathetic *wounded* gazelle, the one the other gazelles abandon while the lions rip at its throat and lick its bones clean. The most humiliating part of this is that the lions at my high school are these white-trash inbreds whose greatest expectations in life are to fill gas tanks or deep-fry burgers. They're morons who I wouldn't trust to tie their own shoes, so believe me, it's no heartache not to be their friends. But sometimes I think it might be nice to go to the movies with someone besides my father.

I mean, it's not like I don't have options. There would be space for me at the misfit table if I wanted it—I could eat my lunch with the nosepickers and the kids who talk to themselves and that guy who tries to set the school on fire every Monday after homeroom. I don't, however. I'd rather be alone than admit my fellowship on the lowest tier of the high-school hierarchy. So instead I bring my father's copy of *The New Yorker* to the cafeteria and read movie reviews or fiction while I eat my sandwich, and if someone tries to push over my table or spill something on my *New Yorker*, I ignore it, because that's the best way to deal with bullies.

But once this blowjob rumor got started it made things really difficult for me when I tried to eat my lunch. I make these elaborate sandwiches for myself, since they give me something to look forward to during the day: goat cheese and fig on brioche, peppered salami on Italian loaf. Two weeks ago, I was sitting in the cafeteria eating ratatouille on sourdough when I felt the black presence of Hill's starting linebacker and resident pre-hominid, Scott Oliver.

"Hey, fatso," he said, leaning over my magazine "What the fuck are you eating?"

Oh, dear. "Ratatouille," I said. My voice was softer than I wanted it to be

"Rata-what?" Scott leaned in close, and his breath could have wilted an acre of flowers. "Rata-vomit?"

"Ratatouille," I whispered again, looking down.

"Hey, fatso—you're eating vomit for lunch again? Is that it? Vomit?"

My next tactic was to ignore him—students at my high school have very short attention spans, and if you ignore them they get bored and disappear. But Scott had an audience. The entire football team was sitting at the table behind him, cheering him on and waving napkins in the air as though this were a pep rally. It seemed I wasn't going to get off easy.

"It's called ratatouille," I said.

"Yeah?" Scott got even closer, his large fleshy head becoming blurry with proximity. "Well, I think it's called vomit." And with that, he took my sandwich, overturned it, and smeared the ratatouille all over the Formica cafeteria table. Then he smiled at me with bovine pleasure, and behind him his teammates cheered as if they'd just won the regionals. It's so embarrassing that *this* is what passes for entertainment at my school.

Well, I accepted the fate of my lunch with dignity and went back to examining my *New Yorker*. I assumed the worst was over; usually a little sandwich destruction keeps the children amused for the rest of the period, and they leave me alone. Unfortunately, on this particular day Scott Oliver was so thrilled with himself and his "vomit" witticisms that he decided to try to impress his teammates with a little off-the-cuff banter.

"Hey, fatso!" he called, loud enough to be heard by everyone but the lunch monitor. "I heard you like to suck dick!" His buddies chortled happily. "I sure wish you'd come over here now and suck mine!" The teammates truly broke up at this point, doubling over with laughter as though Scott were the next Oscar Wilde.

Now, I knew there was no point in getting upset, and I also knew that the closest most of these clowns would ever come to oral sex was in their wettest dreams. But still, I felt angry. Even embarrassed. My cheeks burned, and I stared down at the magazine on my lap like I was trying to see through it. I stayed that way, frozen, until several minutes after the lunch bell rang and it was time to go to French.

The next few days passed in much the same manner. On Tuesday, Scott attempted to entertain the madding crowds with a repeat performance of his sandwich caper. On Wednesday, Curt Malosky, who's considered quite suav-ay because he once met Cindy Crawford in an elevator, stuck a piece of paper on my back that said, "Dick Sukker." I kid you not when I tell you that "Sukker" was spelled with two *k*'s.

But I went about my business, going to classes, eating my lunch, and, at the final bell, getting the hell out of there. At night I would do my homework, read some novel, and have dinner with my dad. I would do my best not to think about the next day, or the day after, or the day after that. My evenings were mine. I never went anywhere near the A&P.

On Friday, after last period, I made the huge mistake of spending too much time at my locker before making my escape. Someone had stuck a giant rubber tube in there, painted pink and affixed, at the bottom, to two pink-painted tennis balls. The result wasn't so much phallic as confused.

I heard clickety footsteps coming up behind me and got nervous. I wasn't sure why some weeks were tougher than others; all I knew was that this week had been extra painful and it was minutes away from being over. Clickety footsteps were not good. They were the kind of footsteps that could keep me from safety and home.

"Hey, fatso." I knew the voice before I turned around. It was Deanna Jeter, who was, of course, the most popular girl in school. It seems that most societies need to appoint themselves dictators, and the greater members of Hills High had decided to elect Deanna. And I must admit that in this particular decision the huddled masses had made a worthy choice. Deanna was gorgeous, which is to say she was blond, blue-eyed, large-breasted, and small-hipped. She was guarded, cool, and sassy, and she smelled like Obsession and nicotine. She was perfect.

What was most remarkable about Deanna Jeter was that although academically as unfit as most of her peers, she managed her kingdom with Machiavellian grace. She pitted friends against each other, destroying any potential competition for her crown. She had been known to reduce cheerleaders to tears with just a sharp sideways look. And Deanna could manipulate men just as easily, for she chose boyfriends to match her whims and dropped them seasonally: blonder, more Nordic types during the winter, and strong, outdoorsier guys come summer. She was currently dating Scott Oliver, he of the strong breath and Neanderthal features, but I was sure she had her reasons.

"Hey, fatso," she said again, and I turned around slowly. As terrifying as Scott or Curt could be, nothing could match the knee-knocking fear of being tortured at Queen Deanna's court.

"Yeah?" I asked, trying not to slump. I could feel myself backing into my locker.

"You suck dick, huh?" she said. Her voice wasn't accusing—it was almost matter-of-fact—and it was strange to hear a coarse word like "dick" emerge from her perfect butterfly lips.

I shook my head and looked down. It was hard to speak.

"No, really, fatso. Tell me the truth. I've heard the rumors anyway. I know what you do."

"No, I . . ." I looked anxiously from side to side, but it was a Friday afternoon. The hallways were deserted. "I don't . . ."

"Listen, if you don't tell me the truth, I'll destroy you." Again, she sounded totally detached, like she was reporting on the lunch specials at the cafeteria. "I'll fucking destroy you."

"Okay," I said.

"Okay?" she said.

"I did it," I whispered.

"I know you did," Deanna said, and she took a step back. "I know. Come with me."

So because this was Queen Deanna, pride of the lionesses, I followed her out to the back hallway and onto the gravel that separated the high school from the athletic fields. While

I watched, hands trembling in my pockets, she fished something out of her knapsack. Lipstick? Cigarettes? A weapon?

No. In her pink, manicured hand was a cucumber, peeled and wrapped in a plastic baggie.

"Huh?" I said.

"Show me how." Deanna extended the baggie-wrapped cucumber, looking straight at me. "I need to know how."

It took me an entire second to figure out what she was talking about—show her what? Show her how? But then, suddenly, a cartoon light-bulb turned on above my head. "Oh my God. Are you kidding?" I asked.

"Do I look like I'm kidding?" she asked back.

Well, I was fifteen years old and I thought the world could no longer shock me, but I was wrong. Deanna Jeter was asking *me* to show *her* how to perform fellatio. I mean, truth be told, I had no negotiating power—I could deny her this favor as easy as the bleeding gazelle could deny the lions its meat. But still—Queen Deanna was asking me for something, and she had resorted to desperate tactics. I had never felt more important in my life. The only problem, of course, was that I had no idea what to tell her. I had never given a blowjob before.

"Show me," she said again, and reached out with the cucumber.

"Ummm . . . okay." I would have to wing it. I took the cucumber from her and unwrapped it, slowly. We were staring at each other, and I'm not sure who was more embarrassed. Deanna was blushing as pink as her Mauve Crystal lipstick, and I could feel sweat rings start to dampen my underarms. "Well," I said, "you just sort of stick it in your mouth, like this." And then I took a breath, and put the cucumber in my mouth, as far back as it would go. Then I slid it out.

Deanna nodded, and crossed her arms across her boobs, like she was protecting something.

I was holding the cucumber in my right hand, thinking to myself, *improvise, improvise!* "You have to be careful not to bite down," I said, because that seemed like an obvious thing. Then, to make the point clear, I pushed the cucumber back down my throat again and then took it out, quickly. "Like that."

"Like that?" Deanna asked. She looked really upset. "You have to stick it that far back?"

"Well, you don't have to," I said. "But if you want it to be good . . . " This was actually kind of fun.

"And you're like, what, like lying on top of them or they're sitting on you, or what?"

"Oh, I don't know," I said. The cucumber was slimy and cold in my fingers. "I guess you could do it either way."

"Oh," Deanna said. She dropped her head and extended her hand, and I gave her back the cucumber. We just stood like that for a moment, shuffling the gravel under our feet.

"Well," she said, after what felt like a year. "Thanks."

"Hey," I said. "No problem."

"Listen, don't tell anyone."

"Oh, I wouldn't."

"I mean it."

"So do I. I won't tell anyone."

"Yeah," she said, and stuck the cucumber back in her bag. She looked up at me again and sort of smiled, sort of smirked, and then she nodded, and then she turned around and walked away.

I guess I shouldn't have expected anything more than that. I spat the taste of cucumber out of my mouth, turned around, and headed home.

|||| Satellites or Airplanes ||||

THERE ARE SEVEN OF US in the kitchen, which is six people too many, but I'm busy trying to keep the potatoes from burning and I don't have the energy to kick anyone out. There's Leigh, and her boyfriend Danny, and the twins, and Catherine, and the Little Man, who's sitting in a corner on a stool, scratching a scab on his knee while the mayhem circles around him. It's a Brooklyn townhouse kitchen, not tiny but not spacious, and since there's a playroom and a garden and a very comfortable living room I don't know what they're all doing in here. It's not like they don't have options.

"Butter," says Leigh, who's careful about such things. "I don't like to see you using so much butter."

"I don't like you watching me cook," I say, and try to shoo her out. "Why won't you people go somewhere else?"

"Go somewhere else, people," Leigh commands, as the twins spill their Japan-jacks on the floor and start playing.

"Go somewhere else," Catherine repeats. She's sitting at the kitchen table, painting her nails, not looking up. Of all of us, Catherine is taking the longest to recover. She still hasn't gone back to school, won't go out, doesn't really eat. She paints her nails a lot or sits quietly with the Little Man, watching television. She's nineteen years old but her eyes already have deep circles under them. I told our father that we should probably send her to a psychiatrist, and although I think he agreed, he never did anything about it.

Tonight's our father's birthday, and I want to make him a dinner that he'll like, but I don't want to overdo it or make something our mother would have made. It's his second birthday without her, but the first one came three weeks after she died and we didn't celebrate. We didn't even remember, actually, until two weeks too late, and though we tried to make it up to him with a small cake and some presents, he only smiled weakly. It was his sixtieth, and I guess we should have remembered, but everything that year was so hard.

"Sixty-one," says Leigh, sticking a fork into the potatoes. I'm sautéing them with mushrooms and bacon and onions; they smell great. "I can't believe our dad's such an old man."

"Get your paws out of my potatoes, Leigh," I say.

"Did you use bacon?"

"Get out."

"Come on, Danny," Leigh says. "We're not wanted."

Danny is crouched on the floor with the twins, watching them play Japan-jacks. He and Leigh will graduate from high school next month and go on to college on separate coasts, but Leigh says she's not upset. She says she's used to separation. "I'm playing," Danny says.

"He's not playing," says Mariel, one of the twins. "He's just *observing*."

"Well, maybe you could all play, or observe, or whatever, somewhere else. I can't breathe in this kitchen. I can't think."

"But it smells so *delicious!*" Donovan, the other twin, says. "It smells like *Mommy's* cooking."

Oh no. I will not let them sucker me like this.

"I'm sorry, people. Everybody out."

"I hate it when you're so freakin' bossy," Mariel sighs, scooping up the jacks. "You're not the boss, you know."

"As far as you're concerned, I am. Pick up all your jacks. If I slip on one, I will be extremely dissatisfied."

"You really aren't the boss," Donovan says, repeating his sister. The twins get stuck on certain toys or foods or ideas and will not let them go. It seems to me that they act more childishly now than they did when they were nine. But then again, this may be normal behavior for twelve-year-olds, I don't know. I don't remember being twelve at all. Twelve was centuries ago.

Danny and Leigh and the twins troop out, spilling jacks along the way, and I can hear them start to argue in the living room about whether or not to turn on the TV or listen to the new Fatboy Slim CD. I hear Donovan call Mariel "assface," and then I hear Mariel call Donovan, "dorkwad," and then I hear the blare of the *Simpsons* theme song, which means the boys must have won the argument.

Catherine is still painting her nails silver. The Little Man still sits on his stool in the corner, watching me cook.

"What else?" he asks.

"What else what?"

"For dinner," he says. He has a very commanding voice for a ten-year-old and never succumbs to any of the babyish tics or whininess that plague the twins.

"Leg of lamb," I say. "Parsley salad. Vichysoisse."

"Cake?" the Little Man asks.

"In the fridge. I ordered it from the Red Hen."

"Carrot," the Little Man says. "With cream-cheese frosting."

"Of course," I say, and leave the potatoes for a moment to kiss him on top of the head. Of all the siblings, he is my favorite.

We put six candles on the cake, and Leigh and Mariel present it with a great deal of singing and clatter, and then we give Dad his gift, a new touring bike. He seems as happy as he's been all year.

Our father is a handsome sixty-one, with lots of gray hair and bright blue eyes. His nose is crooked from being broken so many times; when he was a young man, he used to play baseball and football and box. Dad is a successful tax lawyer and a charming person, reserved but friendly. Dignified. He will be dating again shortly, I'm sure. The women will come lined up around the block, offering pure maple syrup, cottages on Nantucket, degrees in art history. These kinds of women especially think our father is a real catch.

We sit in our usual seats: my dad at one end of the table, Catherine on his left, Leigh on his right. Danny sits next to Leigh, and then on his other side is the Little Man, wearing a bright orange sweatshirt that says "Turbo Happy Monkey Wrestler." My father bought the sweatshirt for him as a gift last year in Tokyo, never expecting that the Little Man would actually wear it. But he does, almost every day, and I think my dad finds this amusing. He seems never to know what to expect from his children, or how close to get to us, or how to predict us.

On the other side of the table sit the twins, blond-haired, freckled, Donovan in plastic-framed glasses, Mariel in wire-rims. They squirm on the hard-backed chairs that my mother found at an antiques show in Bedford—unlike Catherine and the Little Man, they've never learned how to be good, to sit still. I sit at the other end of the table, near the kitchen, opposite my dad. From here, I can keep my eyes on my family but also get to the food quickly, so that everything's served when it's ready and hot.

Dinner was good—the lamb rare and thin-sliced, served with a mint sauce whose recipe I found in one of my mother's old cookbooks. I got the idea for the vichysoisse off the Food Network, and the potatoes were my own creation. It crosses my mind, with a certain amount of both guilt and pride, that my mother's dinners were never this flawless. Some parts of her meals were inevitably either undercooked or burnt. She's been dead for a year, and I wonder: should grief have edited my memory so that only the good things remain? Am I disloyal—or worse, unloving—because I haven't forgotten that when she was in charge, the kitchen was often sloppy, that the Little Man left scattered laundry in the playroom, that the twins once went for two weeks without a bath?

"Cynthia!"

"Sorry, what?"

Leigh is smiling at me. "We were just saying what a good cook you are."

"A born domestic," Catherine says, and I can feel my cheeks turn red.

"I'm not a born domestic," I say.

"Of course you're not," my father says. Where my father grew up, "domestic" meant "maid."

"Just an excellent cook," Danny says.

"Me? No. Well, thanks, but I'm not really."

"I believe you are," Dad says, which settles it. He pulls a cigar out of his Brooks Brothers pocket. "Would anyone like to join me in the garden for a smoke?" He knows Catherine smokes, and so does Danny, and even though cancer runs through our family like left-handedness runs through others, our dad considers tobacco one of life's great pleasures. He wouldn't deny it to any of us.

"I will," says Danny.

"I'll help Cynthia clean," says Catherine, but I rush to protest.

"No, don't be silly. Go join Dad. I'm fine cleaning up. The twins will help."

"We're not helping," Donovan says, but I give him a dark look and he picks up a plate. "I *hate* always having to help."

Catherine sighs, still looking blank, and disappears out to the garden. Once she leaves, I turn to my charges. "Okay, Mariel, Donovan, you guys finish the table. Leigh, I want you to help me load the dishwasher. Little Man—" The Little Man looks up at me, his face round and calm. "Little Man, why don't you go outside and relax with Dad."

"I'd rather sit here," the Little Man says.

"Okay," I say. I can't deny him anything. "Sit there. That's fine."

That night, after the dishes are done and the Little Man is in bed and the twins are in the playroom and my father's taking a birthday stroll through the Heights with Danny and Leigh, I sit at the kitchen table with Catherine, drinking tea.

"So that went well," I say, hoping she'll agree.

"The food was good," she says bluntly, not necessarily an agreement but not necessarily a disagreement, either.

"Well, I think that Dad was touched, anyway."

"Did you know he's fucking his secretary?"

I practically spit out my tea. "What? How do you know that?"

Catherine smiles a little. She likes being able to shock me. She pushes her hair out of her face and says, "It's a little prosaic, I know. I mean, of all people to start fucking, picking your secretary is kind of lame, I think."

"How do you know this, Catherine?"

"I don't for sure," she says, and blows on her tea. "I'm just guessing, actually."

"Well, that's a stupid thing to guess."

"Why would you care?"

"Dad's not the type."

"Don't you think he should be sleeping with somebody, though? I mean, Mom's been underground for like a year."

"Don't talk like that," I say, annoyed. "Don't say she's 'underground.'"

"Well, what would you call it?"

"Dead," I say. "Just say she's dead."

"He's got to be fucking somebody," Catherine says again, dripping some honey into her tea. "He's a red-blooded American male. Besides, he's been so damn chipper lately."

"So?"

"So what makes men happy?"

"I don't know, Catherine," I say. She wears me out so easily. "I really don't know."

"Fucking," Catherine says. "That's pretty much it. But since there've been no phone calls, no family introductions or anything, we've got to assume he doesn't have a proper girlfriend. So if he doesn't have a proper girlfriend, then he's probably just screwing someone on the sly, some dumb chick with no expectations."

"You're jumping to tremendous conclusions."

"And who would have no expectations at all? Who would demand nothing from our poor old dad?"

"Catherine," I say, trying to sound like I'm warning her.

"His secretary!" she announces, like Sherlock Holmes making the final deduction. "Got to be his secretary."

"Which one?" I challenge.

Catherine sighs. "I don't have all the answers just yet," she says. "But I will."

"I think you're an idiot," I say, and stand to dump out my tea.

"I think you're jealous," she says with a little smile.

When they come back from their walk I am waiting on the front stoop. Danny and Leigh go inside, but Dad sits down next to me. His sleeves are rolled up, and he smells like cigar smoke. "Thanks for dinner, Cyn," he says.

"You're welcome," I say. Even though I don't believe a word of what Catherine says, I still want to ask him. It's none of my business, of course. I don't even care, really, but I still kind of want to know for curiosity's sake. But just before I can get the question out, he speaks.

"So you remember Jim from my office? He owns a couple of small buildings in Greenwich Village. He told me one of his apartment's come up for rent, said he'd be glad for you to have it."

"What?" I ask. Why would I want an apartment in Greenwich Village?

"Well, you're twenty-three years old, honey. Don't you think it's time you had a place of your own?"

"You need me here," I say. He's never brought this up before.

"I think we'll get along okay," Dad says, and chuckles again, still sounding all warm and friendly. "Look, honey, I love having you here. You're such a help with the kids, the house. I really appreciate everything you've done. But you have a college degree, right? You want to go to law school, right?"

"That can wait, Dad. I really think I'm needed here." And just for a second, I imagine Dad's secretary, the younger one, all blond and stupid. I imagine her moving into the town-house, making lunch for the Little Man, watching the twins' soccer games, cooking birthday dinners.

"I don't think this situation is fair to you, honey. I think it's time that you moved out. I told Jim that we'd take the apartment."

"I don't want an apartment in Greenwich Village, Dad." I can't believe he wants to replace me.

"It's nice, Jim says. A real one-bedroom, on Perry Street. There's a doorman and a fireplace, oh, and what else, I think he said hardwood floors."

"I don't want it."

My dad sighs. "Your mom would want you to have your own life, Cyn," he says. That's always the trump card, what Mom would want.

"I do have my own life, Dad," I say, hugging my knees to my chest. "And I really think I'm needed here."

He's silent for a moment, and then he coughs into his fist. "I told Jim we would take it," he says again. "I think it's time."

Around two in the morning, alone in the kitchen, I open the window and look up into the sky. We rarely see stars; the bright lights from Manhattan usually drown them out. But I've looked for stars over the garden ever since I was a little girl, after my mother took me to the Hayden Planetarium to teach me about constellations. And tonight, for the first time in a while, I think I can see the North Star, and maybe Orion's belt. I want to show the Little Man.

The lights are out in the hallway, but I can make out the lines in the Picasso drawing that hangs near the stairwell. It's a sketch of a girl holding flowers, a girl I always think is smiling at me. I smile back at her like I always do, and then tiptoe up the dark wood stairs to the room the Little Man shares with Donovan. I can hear Danny and Leigh making out in the living room.

"Little Man," I whisper, outside the door. Like Catherine and me, the Little Man is an insomniac, which is a slightly pathetic condition for a ten-year-old. "Are you up?"

He pokes his sad, round face outside the door. "Of course," he says.

"Come outside," I say. "You can see stars."

"All right," the Little Man says. He's wearing old man's pajamas, a blue striped set just like Dad wears. I'm in a nightgown and a quilted robe, my hair knotted up in a bun. I'm wearing my ugly black glasses. I think to myself that I'm doing a stupid, sentimental thing, dragging my little brother out into the garden like this, past the middle of the night. But I march him downstairs anyway and out the back door. It's cool out, springtime; the roses I planted last summer are starting to bloom in bright pink whirls under the motion-detecting lights.

"Well?" the Little Man says to me, expectantly.

"Orion's belt," I say, pointing. "Can you see it up there?"

"I guess," he says, and pauses. "We're having International Day at school next week. I need you to make me a costume."

"Of course," I say, and try again. "Can you see the stars?"

"Barely," the Little Man says. "I think maybe they're just satellites or airplanes or something."

"No," I say, and tilt his head up and to the right. He has the smoothest skin, baby's skin really, and I think it's a shame that in a few years his face will toughen and grow prickly with stubble. "It's Orion's belt. Up there and to the right. I'm sure."

"I want to be an Arab," he says. "Can you make me a burnoose?"

"Of course," I say again, frustrated. "Just look at the stars."

The Little Man sighs. I stand behind him, my hands still on his face. In a few years, the Little Man won't let me touch him anymore, won't come outside to the garden just to see some vague constellations. He won't need me to make him costumes, or make him lunch, and I guess that that's when I'll know it's time for me to leave.

"Maybe they might be real stars," he concedes. "They might be more than airplanes."

"They might be Mom," I say, startling myself, because I don't really believe our mother is in the heavens, watching us, although sometimes I wish I could.

The Little Man will have none of it. "Oh, please, Cynthia," he says, turning around. He crosses his thin arms on his thin little chest. "Don't say that for *my* benefit."

"I'm not," I say, and push my glasses up my nose. We look at each other for a minute, his round blue eyes narrow with ten-year-old contempt. To make peace, I say, "I know you're too smart for that."

"Good," he says, and drops his arms. He turns and looks up at the stars again, and feels, perhaps, a little sorry for me. He decides to be generous. "Well, maybe it is Mom," he says softly. "Up near the middle star in the belt. Look, the one that's flickering."

"That's the one," I say, feeling silly. I shouldn't force him to indulge me. Our mother is in a family plot upstate. "I'll make you a burnoose tomorrow."

"Okay," he says, and takes my hand. We walk back into the house. "Thanks."

On the Side

IT'S NINE O'CLOCK on a Saturday night and Laura Weissblum, fire of my loins, object of my passions, woman whom I spent eight months wooing and three years doing the dishes for, is sitting on the bed with a tissue stuck up her left nostril, wearing a dirty T-shirt that says "Ginger Rogers did everything Fred Astaire did, only backwards and in high heels."

"I do not love you anymore," I say to her softly in my high-school French. *"Je ne t'aime plus."*

"What?" she asks. Her voice is hoarse and froggy; she brushes a stringy piece of blondish hair out of her eyes. "My ears are all clogged. I can't hear anything."

"You are not the woman you once were," I continue. *"Tu n'es plus la meme femme."*

"You want to order Italian food?" she says to me. She brushes the same sly piece of blondish hair out of her face; her hair is always undisciplined, even when she's healthy and fresh from the beauty salon. She blinks a couple times, hard, to loosen the mucus that has crusted up the corners of her eyes.

"*Tu n'es plus belle*," I tell her, but she's tuning out.

The room smells like Vapo-Rub and Halls cough drops and sweat, and it's too hot. I sit in the ratty wicker rocking chair in the corner, slowly rocking back and forth while Laura dozes periodically, leaning up against the headboard. When she wakes, she looks at the novel in her lap, not at me.

"Were you planning on going out tonight?" she asks after a while.

"Going out? Like out dancing or to the movies or in search of a fine meal?"

"No," Laura sighs. "Out to Rite Aid."

"Do you need me to go to Rite Aid, my sweet?"

"I think I'm out of Halls," she says, and gestures to the nightstand. In fact, I know for sure that she's out of Halls. I ate the last one while she was sleeping.

"Would you like me to get you some more Halls, my sweet?"

"Could you?" she asks. "And not be so smarmy about it?"

I get up from the chair and feel it rock back violently behind me. "Be right back," I say, and she snuggles down under the comforter. Her novel falls onto the rug next to the bed. "*Meme que je ne t'aime plus.*"

"Thanks, hon," she croaks to me from the bedroom as I search around the hall for my keys.

Laura and I marked our third wedding anniversary last month, and since then I've been feeling a little restless. It's not that I've been lusting after other women, necessarily, and it's not that Laura has changed in any fundamental or uncomfortable way. She's still practical and serious and dryly funny, and she still has a frisky side that appears at the strangest moments, like at book parties or academic conferences. But recently, maybe since we bought the apartment in Park Slope, I've started worrying that Laura no longer takes me seriously as a partner or a life-mate. It's the little things she does—tapping her nails on the kitchen table while we're having a conversation, falling asleep so soon after sex that I fear she's actually fallen asleep *during*. She strolls around the apartment, making tea, reading a book, looking so settled—so comfortable. And I've begun to fear that she'd be this settled or comfortable whether or not I shared the house with her. Whether or not I was even around at all.

I've tried talking to Laura about this, and she says I need to get a real job. What kind of job, I've asked her. She says, one that interests me. The problem here is, I've thought about it, and really nothing seems to interest me anymore. I've got my Ph.D., and I've been spending the past three years trying to write a book about science and religion. I've got two titles in my head: *The Religion of Science* and *The Science of Religion*. Either one might appeal to me on any given day. Meanwhile, Laura has risen up the ranks at her academic press, first doing publicity, then getting a job in editorial, then getting an even bigger job in editorial. None of which comes as a surprise. As I've said, or as I've meant to say, Laura is funny and beautiful and exceptionally bright. So she's climbed up her academic press ladder and made enough so we could get this apartment, and I'm still trying to figure out whether or not science is a religion or the other way around.

Last week, I started looking for a job, but then Laura got sick, and I put the search on hold to take care of her. This week, taking care of her has been my full-time job.

Anyway, our third wedding anniversary: we celebrated at the Thai restaurant around the corner from our new place. Over curried chicken and cheap white wine, she asked me if I thought marriage agreed with me, and I told her that, much to my surprise, it did. I wasn't lying.

"Why does that surprise you?" she asked.

"I don't know," I said. "I'm a man. Monogamy isn't supposed to be part of my biological code." Laura raised a blond eyebrow at me, and I decided to do my tough-guy thing. "I was pretty sure," I said, my voice low and confidential, "that I'd get itchy after a year and have to go find some action on the side."

"Did you?" Laura asked, scooping up coconut rice with her chopsticks. "Find some action on the side?"

"Of course not," I said, startled. Laura rarely took my tough-guy thing seriously. "Are you kidding?"

"Well, I didn't think you had," she said, grinning through a mouthful of rice. "But there's no harm in asking."

"What do you mean there's no harm in asking? There's lots of harm in asking. It shows you don't trust me."

"You're the one said you thought you'd cheat after a year," she pointed out. "I was just checking."

"I'm offended," I said.

"Oh please," she said, and smirked. "It was just a question." Then she turned her attention back to her chopsticks and began picking up grains of rice, one at a time. I watched her for a moment, feeling slightly unsettled, and then I coughed. She didn't say anything. I coughed again.

"No, Greg," she said, finally, putting her chopsticks down next to her plate and giving me a bemused smile. "I've never gotten any on the side, either."

"I wasn't going to ask that," I said.

"Yes you were," she said, remaining bemused. "Eat your dinner and relax."

"I wasn't going to ask that," I repeated, flustered. Because really, I wasn't.

But now that she'd brought it up, was it on my mind? Was it a question worth asking? I mean, as long as it was out there I couldn't help considering it. I'd be a fool not to. Laura was a sexy woman in her own bookish way, and I'd been with her long enough to see the way that men responded to her and to see how she responded to them. A little laugh, a pat on the bicep, a smile that stayed on her face for a few beats after the man in question disappeared. Did I think she'd ever cheated on me? God, no—I mean, I hoped not. I couldn't bear to think about it. Could she?

No. Not my Laura.

But the question stayed with me longer than I wanted it to, and I began, predictably, to imagine her flirting with other men while she was at work, or giggling with her friends over some bartender's cute ass, or staying on the phone much longer than necessary with my brother whenever he called. Soon I was imagining her fucking these men, sleeping with her boss or her sister's husband or some random guy she met at a book party. Perhaps I was being unfair.

Perhaps I wasn't.

God, how I wished she'd never brought it up in the first place.

Tonight it's warm out for September, and I take my time walking to the Seventh Avenue Rite Aid. The buildings on our block are all nineteenth-century townhouses, many with small gardens and fancy mailboxes out front. Some of them have been separated into apartments, like our building, but most are still single-family homes, and their windows are full of children's drawings or warm, living-room light. I stop in front of one of the houses near the corner and try to peek in, because I've passed this house before and seen a good-looking fortyish woman vacuuming in her bra. Tonight her curtains are shut, but I stand in front of her house for a minute anyway, thinking that maybe she'll open the curtains and do a little naked Saturday-night housecleaning. It's possible.

Laura doesn't clean. It was part of the deal we made when I proposed. I said, Laura, will you marry me? And she said, Of course I will. If. If what? I asked. If you agree to always do the dishes, and make the bed, and clean the bathroom. Especially clean the bathroom, she said. I hate that.

I asked her if we could hire a maid, and she said sure, when we could afford it. Seeing as how, at the time, she was the sole publicity person at her academic press and I was working on my dissertation, it didn't seem likely that we were going to hire a maid very soon.

"I have to do the dishes?" I asked.

"Yes," she said. "But I'll balance the checkbook and make breakfast and when the time comes, I'll push out the babies."

"Fair enough," I said, and we agreed to get married and did so the next week, at City Hall.

I wonder now, staring at the home of the half-naked vacuumer, if Laura would have married me even if I hadn't agreed to wash the dishes. I like to think she would have.

After five minutes or so the vacuumer's curtains are still shut, and so I turn and continue down our street. Folks are out, walking dogs or holding hands or both. I've always been too interested in other people—I stare a lot and get in trouble for it—and I can feel myself doing it now, walking so slowly that I'm barely moving, looking at my neighbors scattered about the sidewalks with their apple-cheeked kids and their ugly pets and their girlfriends. There's a guy smoking a cigarette on the stoop across the street from where I'm standing, wearing a denim jacket, shaggy haircut. I can tell he's brooding through his cigarette smoke and I think to myself, I bet that guy gets laid all the time. The guy stubs out his cigarette and lights up a new one, and I think, yes sir, that guy gets laid all the time.

And in a moment, I'm at that great dreadful pause on the top of a roller coaster. My heart slows, my palms sweat . . . and suddenly—bam!—I'm on my way, watching this guy fuck my wife. First he's on top of her, then underneath, and then behind. He's pumping, she's laughing, they're shimmying on top of each other in some sort of weird copulation breakdance. She's moaning a lot, and her forehead is wrinkled and shiny like it gets when she's about to come. And then, with a grunt and a heave, he's done, and then she's done, and the image dissolves into nothing but a dull red ache in my brain.

Oh, God.

Strange men having sex with my wife. The idea has haunted me lately, and once I start thinking about it I'm held hostage until they've both climaxed, sometimes more than once, and lit up their post-coital cigarettes. No matter how I try, I can't force the image up and away. Worse, perhaps, is that I've been able to see the fucking from all sides— wide view, close-up, looking down from above as though I were a mirror on a whorehouse ceiling. And believe me, nothing about it turns me on. There's no illicit thrill in watching some stranger doing my wife from behind. But I keep coming back to it anyway, any time I meet a guy who seems wealthy or good-looking or confident at all. Like the guy across the street. In the denim jacket, with the shaggy haircut.

Who finishes his second cigarette and flicks it out toward where I'm standing. I stand up straight and square my shoulders, trying to send a signal that he better not mess with me, that he better stay away from my wife.

"Is there a problem?" he calls out to me. He's got a deep kind of fuck-you voice.

"No problem," I say, trying to make my voice come from deep in my chest, so that I sound fuck-you too.

"You're looking at me funny," he says.

"No," I say, quickly and much to my embarrassment, my voice breaks. It does that sometimes, when I'm trying to make my voice come from deep in my chest. I hope the guy hasn't heard. I turn my head and walk quickly down the street, toward Seventh Avenue. I think that maybe he'll call after me, say something threatening or rude, but he doesn't, and I'm grateful.

The Rite Aid is still open. Neon-lit, oversized, proudly utilitarian, the drugstore sticks out like a cellblock among its stately Victorian and Brooklyn brownstone neighbors. On its left is a pet store called The Bow Wow Club. On its right is The Park Slope Ice Cream and Confectionary Shoppe. I zip my jacket up to my neck because the Rite Aid tends to be cold, and then walk in like a king through the automatic doors, which have spread themselves open just for me. Now that I'm three blocks away from the guy on the step, the groove is back in my stride.

Halls. Sure, I can get Halls. And while I'm at it, I toss in a big pink bag of Ricola cough drops, and some Sudafed, and some Tums, just in case. I'm carrying a blue plastic bin under my arm like I'm goddamn Little Red Riding Hood and decide that instead of hurrying home to my beloved, I feel like wandering the Rite Aid aisles and seeing what else the store has to offer. Maybe I'll buy myself a gift.

Walking leisurely past the fluorescent-bright shelves, I note that my local drugstore stocks paper towels, staple removers, and boxy cans of pre-ground coffee. I could purchase film, hairdryers, razors, or air fresheners; also toilet cleaner, mascara, and blank video cassettes. Also romance novels. Also pipe tobacco—with a picture on the label of five men in Rembrandt hats and collars smoking animal-horn pipes. Spontaneously, I decide that I need this product, even though I have yet, in my twenty-nine years, to ever smoke a pipe. But I think maybe the tobacco will do me some good. Also, maybe, some apple-essence hair conditioner. And maybe some jumbo beeswax candles shaped like logs. And also—walking down the last aisle, past the enemas, tampons, and cures for vaginal dryness, fewer than ten but no fewer than five feet away from a comely redhead contemplating Playtex—maybe I need a three-pack of Lifestyles Ultrasensitive condoms with spermacide.

Laura is on the pill. Loestrin 21/7—three weeks a month of little beige pills, seven days of little green ones. The green ones, they're just placebos, and sometimes I swallow them myself to amuse her, pop them down with scotch or without any liquid at all. The pills are tiny, and Laura's been taking them forever, since even before we met. She used to get terrible cramps and the pills helped her manage them. She was on the pill when she was a virgin. I used to think that was sexy.

I barely remember using condoms with Laura, although I guess we must have, during that week or so before we decided to throw caution to the wind and start fucking three, four times a night. In that situation, condoms were not at all economical. And they weren't any fun, either, and Laura got all worried about how the latex we were using would affect the environment. To put a stop to all this condom nonsense, I proposed that Laura become my wife eight months after we met. People who are married really shouldn't be using condoms, right? I mean, that would be bizarre. So we didn't, and felt just fine about it.

If I brought home a little gray package of condoms and showed them to her, Laura would think I had totally lost my mind. And if I just stuck them in a drawer for her to come across, she'd hold them to the light like they were an archeological specimen and ask me about them, casually, over dinner. She wouldn't assume I was having an affair—she's made clear that she doesn't have such worries about me. She thinks I'm as as faithful as a toy poodle. And isn't she right? I mean, is she ever anything but right?

But then, just as I'm about to put the condoms back on their little metal hook, my wife pops again into my imagination. This time she's with my brother, sitting naked on top of him, touching her breasts and throwing back her hair and laughing. I shake my head, blink, try to force the picture out of my head, but the harder I try the louder Laura laughs, my brother moving frantically underneath her. "Stop," I say out loud, and the comely redhead looks at me queerly. "Stop," I say again, but Laura won't.

And so, in revenge, I add the Lifestyles to my basket. Then I square my shoulders—I'm the tough guy again—and hurry to go pay for my things.

Outside the store, I stop to tie my shoelace. I'm trying to figure out which way to go home—I don't want to come back the way I came, don't want to see that guy on the stoop again—when a voice behind me says, "Hey. You know a lot about computers, right?"

"Excuse me?" I ask, standing up. It's the comely redhead. She must have seen me buy the condoms. Maybe she—Jesus—maybe she thinks I'm some sort of stud.

"Aren't you the guy who works at A to Z Computing?" she asks, but she's smiling wide with her hands in her pockets and I think to myself, what's she really asking me?

"Actually," I say, "I'm unemployed."

"Oh," the redhead says and looks disappointed for a second. But then she snaps her head back up. "Well, do you happen to know anything about computers? I'm trying to send a fax from my Macintosh, but the whole system's bugging out. And I've been calling customer support and everything . . . are you sure you're not the guy from A to Z? You look just like him."

"Sure I do," I say, nodding casually. I mean, there's every possibility I look like the guy from the computer store, but then there's a certain possibility she's trying to pick me up. I mean, why wouldn't she? I can almost feel the condoms throbbing in their Rite Aid bag. "I'm not the guy you think I am," I say. The redhead looks at me quizzically. "But I do know something about computers." I feel the plastic bag get slippery in my sweaty palm, so I transfer it to the other hand. "Maybe we should . . . I mean, if you want, I guess I could take a look."

"Would you mind?" she says. "That's really nice of you."

"No problem," I say. "No problem at all." We're not exchanging names, but that's all right with me.

We walk down Seventh Avenue and turn onto Garfield, which is, thankfully, not the street of the guy on the stoop, and the redhead makes amiable chitchat about faxing and Macintoshes and how they're supposed to be so easy but they're not. As I walk next to her, I think to myself, what would Laura say if she saw me here? What would my wife think of her unemployed jerk of a husband, her faithful poodle husband, walking casually down Garfield with such a comely redhead? I bet she'd start paying attention. I bet she'd get better in a hurry.

"You know," the redhead says, as we stop in front of her small brick apartment building. "I do appreciate your help— it's ridiculous that I'm so helpless with computers, I can't believe I'm going around Rite Aid looking for tech support . . . " She sticks out her hand and smiles. "I'm Donna."

I shake her hand, which is dry and soft. "I'm . . . " I pause for a minute and consider giving her a fake name, but the only thing I can think of is Valentino, which I seriously doubt she'd buy. "I'm Greg."

"Well, listen, Greg, this is really sweet of you. I mean it." Jesus, maybe she is flirting. Maybe she actually is. The cute little flirty redhead puts her backpack on the pavement and starts rifling through it, looking for her keys, and I can't believe it, but I'm sure she's flirting. She's bending down in front of me; her ass is round and firm in my face, barely hidden behind a flimsy flowered skirt. As she bends, her ass moves up and down, up and down. Oh, shit.

Suddenly I'm on top of the roller coaster again, only this time, I'm seeing me. Me! Me and the redhead, grunting on top of each other, sweating and heaving. Me, flipping her over, her naked and moaning, me driving her crazy with my carnal skill. Me!

By the time she finds her keys, we've both come, twice.

"Got 'em," she says, sticking a bright silver key in the dull metal lock. It's much too much. I can't go through with it, whatever this woman wants. I don't know a damn thing about computers.

As she opens the door, I open my mouth. "I'm sorry," I blurt. "I think you're a nice girl and everything, Donna, but I just can't do this. I'm sorry. Please forgive me."

"What?" the redhead says, still holding the door open. "Well, okay, don't worry about it. Thanks anyway."

"No, thank *you*," I say, "for understanding." And then I pick up the Rite Aid bag in my sweaty hands and scurry home to my sick wife.

"You're back," Laura says. Her voice sounds froggier, and our small bedroom is even steamier than it was before. Laura doesn't seem to notice the heat, however; she's huddled under the puffy green comforter, pulling it up to her neck.

"Are your teeth chattering?" I ask, dropping the Rite Aid bag on the dresser. The room is dark, the curtains shut, but I can still see the faintest chatter in my wife's mouth. It seems perverse that her teeth would chatter in this kind of heat. My neck is sweaty and my pants are sticky and yet my wife's mouth is what seems perverse to me.

"Maybe," she says. "I'm cold."

"How can you be cold? It's a million degrees in here." I go to sit next to her, brushing away the snowdrift of used Kleenex that has collected at her side. I put my hand on her forehead, expecting feverish warmth, but instead it's cold, even clammy, if foreheads can get clammy. "Did you take any aspirin?"

"A half an hour ago. It should kick in soon," she says. Then she takes my hand off her forehead and holds it between her own. "What took you so long?"

My stomach compresses, and I can feel my neck get damper. "It was nice out," I say, trying to get my voice from my chest. "I was strolling."

"Ah," she says, taking in this information without any signs of irritation or disapproval. I know my wife, and she is not the type to ever say, "Strolling? You were strolling when I needed medicine?" Nor would she ever begrudge me a little walk. But even knowing this, I feel guilty, and then resentful that she makes me feel guilty. Even though nothing happened. Really nothing.

"Sorry," I say, and go to the dresser to toss her the Halls. "Here you go."

"Thanks," she says, and closes her eyes.

"Aren't you going to take one?"

"Not now," she says. "My throat doesn't hurt so much anymore. Now I'm just tired."

"Okay," I say, standing in the doorway, my resentment giving way to anxiety, even feistiness. I want her to stay awake, I want to keep her talking, I want her to go look through the Rite Aid bag and find the condoms and be—be what, I don't know. I want her to react. I want her to know what I've been up to.

But instead she just closes her eyes and starts to breathe heavily, and I can hear the air make its labored way through my wife's clogged-up nose. I watch her fall asleep, and then leave her there in the tropical bedroom, closing the door behind me. I think to myself, strangely, that I miss her.

At three in the morning, I wake up with my face pressed against the corduroy pillows of our hand-me-down sofa. I've fallen asleep in the front room, with the television on, sound turned off, and an unopened bottle of scotch pressed underneath me, between the two large sofa cushions. I sit up and hold the scotch bottle in front of me, trying to figure out what woke me up and whether or not I feel like a drink. Then I hear it: a long, painful, lusty cough emerging from the bedroom. It sounds like she's hacking up entire lungs in there. I drop the bottle on the sofa and run.

Laura's sitting up on the bed, an expectant look on her face, and I wonder how long she's been sitting like this, waiting for me to come help. She holds up a tissue to me. "Look," she says, almost proudly. "Blood."

"Blood?" I say, taking a second to pull this all together. Her face is so damn pale. "You're coughing up blood?"

"It's probably nothing," she says—now that she's shocked me she wants to take the shock away, but it's too late. I'm on the phone with 911, giving my wife's health and address details to the operator.

"I don't need an ambulance," she says; with her nose the way it is, the words sound like *I dote deed a dabulass*. I pretend I can't figure out what she's saying as I repeat our address to the operator, and my poor wife says it again, "I dote deed a dabulass. Greg, I dote deed a dabulass."

"Look at this," I say roughly, and hold up a tissue so that she can see her own blood, speckling the phlegm on the Kleenex like a spray of paint.

"I probably just have bronchitis," she says, and I wave my hand at her as the operator confirms where we live. The Methodist Hospital is only a few blocks away. An ambulance should be here shortly—or we could even walk.

"Bronchitis," she says to me again as I hang up the phone. "It's no big deal. I'll go to the doctor tomorrow."

"If you're coughing up blood," I say, "then you should go to the hospital." I can hear it in my voice—I sound like I'm talking to a small, stupid child.

She rolls her eyes at me and gets out of bed, pulling her cardigan close around her and shivering a little. "Great," she says. "Now I have to look decent for the ambulance guys." She grabs a brush off the dresser and runs it through her hair quickly, and I feel a tiny shudder of jealousy rock me and then disappear before I can even remember to ignore it.

"You don't have to look decent for ambulance guys. They're used to sick people."

She ignores me, running the brush through her hair.

"Well, then . . . " I say, "I'll go open the door for the . . . you know . . . " I have to get myself out of there. I need to be away from the bedroom stench and the heat and the blood-sprayed Kleenex and my sick wife brushing her hair for the ambulance guys. She keeps ignoring me, taking off her cardigan and her dirty T-shirt and pulling on a clean sweatshirt from the top drawer. When she strips, her small breasts look unbearably soft and white, and I think to myself that the doctors are going to see her, everyone's going to see her, and I've got to get out of there before I get even crazier.

In a few minutes she joins me by the door. She's still shivering. She's washed her face—I can smell her chamomile soap—and her limp hair is pinned off her face with a silver barrette. It strikes me, as it often does when I'm throbbing with jealousy, that I am married to an exceptionally beautiful woman. She's so much more beautiful than the redhead could ever be. She coughs; I'm surprised by a rush of concern. I put my arm around her shoulders and she tucks into me, shivering, as we wait for an ambulance to come save us.

"*Tout sera bien*," I say to her. It means, I think, that everything will be all right.

Turns out that in the wide battery of accidents and diseases that confront a Brooklyn emergency room on a Saturday night, a Kleenex sprayed with blood means very little. I fill out the paperwork in a shaky hand, and then we wait. For two hours. Laura half-sleeps on a stretcher in the Methodist Hospital emergency room, and I hold her hand and convulse with impatience, guilt, worry. The emergency room is pink and white, calm and clean, but I still feel like I'm exposing Laura to germs, filth, nastiness. I feel like this is all somehow my fault.

When we're finally wheeled into a small examination chamber, the doctor looks at both of us with pity. She's an older Indian woman with large brown eyes and a sweet smile. "Long night," she says to me.

"You know it," I say, sitting down in a metal chair next to the stretcher, still holding Laura's hand.

Laura sits up, breathes, coughs, describes her phlegm, describes the blood, and in about three minutes the doctor has made her diagnosis. "Sinus infection, bronchitis—painful, but not the end of the world."

"That's it?" I ask. "Are you sure? What about the blood?"

"You probably broke a blood vessel coughing so hard," she says, and Laura nods to confirm.

"Are you sure?" I ask. "You don't need X-rays or something? She'll be okay?"

The doctor touches my arm, and Laura smiles slightly. I can see it—my wife is bemused.

"She'll be fine. On some very heavy antibiotics, but otherwise fine." And then a nurse appears with some pills in a Dixie cup, and the doctor writes out a prescription, and we're dismissed with a warning to eat before taking the antibiotics, and to rest. Hustled out of the emergency room without so much as a good-bye.

Outside, the night has become early morning, and it's still warm out. I take Laura's hand to lead her to one of the cabs that line up outside the Methodist Hospital, but she shakes her head.

"Let's walk," she says.

"No, you shouldn't be—"

She takes her hand out of mine. "I want to walk."

So we walk together in silence, down Seventh Avenue, past the sewing shop and the old folks home and The Bow Wow Club and the Rite Aid. I think of the condoms, sitting there in a bag on our dresser, waiting to strike. I think of the redhead. I'm such a jerk.

As we near a corner, Laura starts to lean against me, walking slow. "Are you okay?" she asks after a while.

My sick wife is asking me if I'm okay. I don't respond. Then she nudges me in the side, and finally, I say, "I was worried."

"I know," she says. "I told you not to be."

"I can't help myself," I say.

"You have nothing to worry about," she says, and we make a right onto our street. Laura stops for a minute to catch her breath; we're standing in front of the house of the naked vacuumer.

"A woman who does the cleaning in her underwear lives here," I say, to try and start a fresh conversation.

"Oh," Laura says, and then looks up at me. "Why did you buy condoms?"

"What?"

"They were in the Rite Aid bag," she says, and sits down on the vacuumer's stoop. The sun is coming up, in the bright ripe colors of summer fruit. I can hear the birds begin their frantic early-morning chirps. "The Rite Aid bag on the dresser," Laura adds.

"I know," I say, and then, "I don't know why I bought them." I say this truthfully, because it's been so long since

I've been the tough guy and I really can't tell her why I've done what I've done, or what propels me to act like such an asshole, or why I get such crazy ideas to fly through my imagination like witches on broomsticks. I want to tell her, though, because I want her to know and understand me. Or maybe I want to tell her because she understands me already, and I need her to help me figure myself out.

"Are you looking," she asks between coughs, "for some action on the side?"

"No," I say, truthfully. "Of course not."

"Okay," she says, and I turn to look at her, expecting bemusement, but I don't see any.

"I was just surprised to see the condoms," she says.

"Are you mad?" I ask.

"Should I be?" she says.

"No," I say softly, selfishly.

"I wasn't kidding," she says to me, after a few minutes. "You really don't have to worry about me. I'm not going anywhere."

"Sure," I say, holding both her hands in my own. "I know."

When we get back to our apartment, I open up the windows to allow some fresh air in. Laura takes a shower, and I throw out her dirty tissues, change the sheets on the bed, and put her pills on the bedside stand with a glass of orange juice. Next to the orange juice, I stack her Halls, a bottle of aspirin, and the novel she's been reading since she got sick. After thinking about it for a moment, I throw the Rite Aid bag out the window.

When Laura comes into the bedroom, wrapped in my old bathrobe, she walks over to the wicker rocker and kisses me on the forehead. "I'm completely beat," she says; it sounds like, "I'b copledely bead." Then she takes off the bathrobe and remains naked for several seconds as she pulls pajamas out of the dresser. I guess she's not feeling so cold anymore. But for the first time in three months, I can watch her naked body moving around the bedroom without feeling any anger, disgust, or fear. Instead, I'm caught in pleasant admiration, because my wife is slender and pale and, as I've said several times, extremely beautiful. In fact, when she pulls on fresh pajamas, in blue and white stripes, I'm almost sorry. And as she crawls into bed and swallows her pills, I suddenly have the urge to crawl in next to her, and put my arms around her. So I do.

"*Tout sera bien,*" Laura says to me softly in her own high-school French.

"*Je t'aime,*" I respond. Then we lie there quietly as the day grows brighter, until we eventually both fall asleep.

Hey, Beautiful

I'M SITTING IN THIS BAR with Clare and the girl that Clare brought along, the one in her art class who's supposed to be so great and funny and cosmopolitan. That's a big thing with Clare, that her friends be cosmopolitan, and so sometimes I wonder why she spends all this time with me.

Clare is wearing a short black dress and her friend is in a short black dress and I'm wearing jeans, and I don't smoke and neither does Clare, usually, but tonight she does. The friend, Jeanette, has long red hair and long red nails and lights her own cigarettes, even when a man offers to do it for her. Clare lets the men do it for her.

It's happy hour, Jeannette's favorite three hours of the day. But it's darkening early, late November already, and I'm a senior in college. A senior in college, says a voice in my head, but then I blink, and that ugly thought, and the thoughts that have to follow, go away. We all just turned twenty-one, anyway, and so the three of us sit on matching barstools around a mahogany bar down in the financial district. Jeannette dates men from the financial district, although sometimes she'll go out with a law student. Clare recently broke up with her boyfriend, Tom, because he isn't going into law or finance. Tom wants to be a poet. He smokes a lot of pot and writes poetry about Clare. I don't date that much, but I keep busy.

Clare and I have been suitemates since freshman year, and I guess she feels some sort of allegiance towards me. She sets me up with boys sometimes, or tries to give me fashion advice. At the end of freshman year, she gave me a home perm. She never understood why I stayed in the library so much and I found that I couldn't really explain. Once, after watching a BBC documentary on The Canon, I told her that I loved the feel of books, of heavy covers and leather bindings and dust. I thought this was just the sort of *Masterpiece Theater* thing that might impress her. Clare laughed and told me I needed to go out more. I was indignant. For a while we fought, but things slipped back into routine when I wasn't paying attention.

A man across the bar is making eyes at Clare and she's smiling back, and Jeannette pushes her forward off the stool. "Go on, sweetheart! He's just adorable!"

Clare stands up straight and taps her cigarette on the bar, leaving a small pile of gray ash. She straightens her skirt and tosses her head just a little, and makes her way through the suits and the ties and miniskirts and briefcases, toward the balding man who is, indeed, winking at her.

"You've never been to this bar before, huh?" Jeannette is addressing me and I don't know how to respond. I usually maintain a policy of honesty, but sometimes the truth is embarrassing. I reach for a compromise.

"I've passed it before, but I've never actually had a drink here."

Jeannette smiles compassionately, and so I decide to further complicate my story. "I mean, I've been down to this area, of course, because I love business and I'm really interested in Wall Street, you know. I mean, I major in economics and I think it's all fascinating." Fascinating? Jeannette doesn't use the word "fascinating"; she prefers "fabulous." She keeps smiling at me.

"I've heard the economics program is quite . . . rigorous," she says.

The smoke is thick around us and the television above the bar is broadcasting a Knicks game. The man next to me is holding a beer to his forehead, his tie loose around his neck. I stare at the details, the pattern of a polo player on his button-down shirt.

"I study poetry myself," she continues, talking to the air right above my head. She must sense that I'm thinking about her, my cheeks burning, even though I refuse to look at her. "I love writing. I absolutely do. It's just my calling, you know. Everybody has a calling. Writing is my calling." She lights another cigarette for herself and turns to the bartender. I can hear her order a gin and tonic, and then a man in a green tie whispers something to her. Spinning around in her stool, Jeannette disassociates herself from me.

Well, enough then. I get up off my stool and push my way out of the bar, through the androgynous businesspeople with their beers and their weary postures. I head out under the neon exit sign, and turn left into the silent street named for a wall that once kept the Indians from invading all of civilized Manhattan.

I wasn't lying to Jeannette. I have been to the financial district before. When I was a little girl, my family took a trip to New York. While my mother and sister went to Bloomingdale's, my dad and I went down to Wall Street. We stood in a glass cage above the stock exchange, peered over the men in shirtsleeves and the red sweaty faces and the numbers parading in digital code. I picked up a phone in the little glass cage and heard the codes translated into some Asian language. I assumed it was Chinese.

Eight years later, during my first semester at Columbia, I took Clare down to the financial district and we walked through the narrow streets, some still cobblestoned, and talked about our futures. She wanted to be a lawyer, because she didn't have the patience to be a doctor but she still wanted to make a good living one day. I told her I wanted to study money, and we both felt some sort of kinship.

Later that afternoon, drinking hot chocolate on a stoop near Fraunces Tavern, Clare asked me what I thought of Tom. They had been dating for a few months, she said, and she wasn't sure whether now was the right time to get serious.

"Well, do you like him?" I asked, reviewing what I knew of Tom and trying to figure out what Clare could possibly find wrong.

"He's really sweet to me and everything," she hedged, sipping on her hot chocolate and tracing a pattern on the pavement with the toe of her left Weejun. "But I'm not sure he's the one, you know? I mean, how do I know if he's the one?"

"Well, we're just freshmen," I said, feeling rather important, like a love doctor. "You don't really have to know if he's the *one* or not. But if you ask me, I think he's cool as hell."

Clare stopped with the Weejun and looked up at me, a smirk on her face. "Cool as hell?" she asked.

"You know what I mean," I said, blushing, sure I had given something away. Clare nodded, and then left me there to go back uptown and get serious with Tom.

Alone, I kept walking around the cobblestoned streets, bumping into pigeons and hot dog vendors. I thought about being a girl, how I was never good at being a girl. This isn't to say I was a tomboy, in any nineties girl-power kind of way. I'd always assumed if I were born male, I wouldn't have been that good at being a boy, either. I just couldn't perfect any of the routines associated with youth or adolescence. I liked Clare—I admired her the way you might admire someone else's religion. She was exotic in her own rituals, but I found it hard to believe in her.

I think about that afternoon now as I climb up the stairs of the treasury, the spotlit statue of George Washington behind me. The financial district is dark and quiet at night, with the exception of a few bars and lost taxis. I stare out at the streets for a while and wonder how long it will take Clare and Jeannette to miss me. I imagine a scene:

Clare: I think we finally lost her.

Jeannette: Well, seriously, *darling*, I can't imagine why you spend all that time with her in the first place! I mean, where are her conversation skills? Who on earth does she know in this town? And most importantly, what in God's name was she wearing?

Clare: Seriously, did you get a load of those jeans? Where did she think she was going? The library? (*laughter all around*) You know why I hang out with her? Because I never have to worry that she'll steal all the attention.

Jeannette (inhaling on her cigarette): Oh, good point. (*exhaling*) I mean, really, that's a *fabulous* point.

I shudder and remind myself that they'll probably both end up bitter and face-lifted and divorced. Still, that reminder is no great comfort when it's my ass that's cold and numb on these steps, while they're sitting warm inside, flirting and licking the tops of beer bottles suggestively.

I'm so caught up in making myself feel bad that I don't notice a man sitting next to me on the steps until he says, "Hey, beautiful."

He is wearing a white shirt and a tie and dark pants. He is drinking a can of Coke and sitting about five feet away from me. He is smiling at me.

"Excuse me?"

"I said, 'Hey, Beautiful.'" I stare at him. Does he really think I'm beautiful? Is he a pervert? Or worse, making a joke?

Beautiful.

Before I got in the car that was to take me to the plane to

take me to New York, my mother cried a little and pushed a small paper bag into my hands. "Be careful," she whispered, with the urgency of last words, "and be prepared."

Condoms, a twelve-count, in little foil wrappers. Clare and I made water balloons out of them and lobbed them at our neighbors. Later, she regretted this. "Six bucks for twelve condoms? Are they kidding?" I would shrug, trying to pass off my ignorance as indifference. "Maybe it's better to just get the economy pack."

Then, at the beginning of this semester, when Clare was out dancing at some dance club and the rest of the suite was watching *Ally McBeal* in the common area, I sat in my room and caught up on my Economics of Wartime reading. I was wearing a blue Columbia sweatshirt and my hair was up in a knot on top of my head; I munched on peanut M&Ms from a bowl on my desk. Someone knocked on my door. I said, "Come in!" with my mouth full of crunchy peanut goodness.

The door creaked open, and in staggered Tom, recently broken up with Clare and looking about as bad as I'd ever seen him. His hair, usually so golden and curly, was dull with grease and plastered flat on his forehead. The whites of his blue eyes were veined with red. He smelled like Southern Comfort and body odor.

"Lisa," he said, buckling down to the floor. "You seen Clare?"

"Sorry," I said. "I think she's out dancing or something."

"She with that new guy?"

"New guy?" I said. "I haven't heard of any new guy."

"Yeah . . . sure . . ." Tom slurred. "You're a good girl, Lisa . . . It's nice of you to lie like that."

"No, really," I said. "It's the truth."

"Shit . . ." he moaned, and spread himself out on my floor, on his back, face up. Poor guy. I guess I had always suspected that Clare would ruin him. I'd felt so sorry for him when they were together, the way he chased after her like an orphan, the way he fetched for her like a slave. And he was so handsome, and sweet, in a stupid-hearted way, and sometimes he would leave poetry on our answering machine—stuff he wrote, or else things by Wallace Stevens or Walt Whitman. Depending on who was in the room when she checked her messages, Clare would either listen to the poems and blush, or else erase them before Tom was even finished.

"Tom?" I asked, quietly. "You okay?"

"Of course I am," he said, and rolled over on to his side, coughing.

"You gonna puke?" I asked, reaching under my desk for the bucket we kept for emergencies.

"Nah . . ." Tom said. He lay there on his side then, and didn't say anything, and I tried to go back to my reading, but of course that was impossible. I mean, he was lying there, his flannel shirt open, a curl of golden hair reaching down from his belly button, his eyes half closed, his mouth half open. I could hear his ragged breathing. If he hadn't been drunker than Dionysus, he might have even been sexy.

"Lisa?" he slurred again, and I let my hair out of the knot on my head, and felt it fall straight to my shoulders.

"Tom," I said, "you look terrible. We should get you some water."

"No . . . " He sat up. "I'm all right." Then he looked at me, and his eyes suddenly seemed clearer. "Hey, Lisa?"

"Yeah?"

"You wanna kiss me?"

"Kiss you?" I said. I would have laughed, told him he was drunk and kicked him out running, except that I did want to kiss him, enormously. I wanted to kiss him more than I wanted long red hair or long red nails or an A+ in Economics of Wartime. I had probably wanted to kiss him since the first time Clare brought him home. And so instead of laughing, I got up out of my chair and walked to where he was sitting on the floor. He just watched me, propped up against my bed, his eyes seeming clearer, his breathing more even.

When I got to him, I knelt down and put my mouth against his. His lips were soft and quite warm, and although his breath was terrible I wanted him to open his mouth.

He didn't. Instead, after a moment, he pulled away. "Sorry," he mumbled. "I guess that's not really what I wanted."

My cheeks burned. "Okay," I said. "That's okay."

Tom looked up at me, and I had to look away, but from my peripheral vision I saw him stumble to his feet and out the door. "Sorry," he mumbled again.

So what would Clare say to that?

And now I've almost forgotten this man here, except that he coughs too loudly and I guess that he's still staring at me.

We sit there in silence on the steps. I hear something, and realize it's my watch ticking. Fight-or-flight kicks in, and I'm aware of every breeze, of the noise he makes as he sips his Coke, the way my stomach rumbles. I think, if I can concentrate hard enough, I might even hear new zits pop out on my face.

He coughs a little and takes a swig of his Coke. "Really," he says, "you have a great smile."

I mumble, "Fuck off," under my breath, but either he doesn't hear me or he mishears me.

"I'm sorry, what?" His excuse to move closer. I shift a little the other way and wrap my arms around myself.

"Did you say something?" He has a scratchy voice.

"No."

"Yes, you did. I heard you."

"I didn't say anything." A scene from a fourth grade film about Mr. Stranger Danger appears, quite suddenly, in my head. "Would you like some candy, little girl?" Mr. Danger asks, in a sing-songy voice. "It tastes *good!*"

I blink, and the scene goes away. The man loosens his tie, takes a last loud gulp of Coke, and throws the can into the wastebasket at the bottom of the stairs. Perfect basket.

"Well, it was nice talking to you," he says, getting up off the stairs. He's cute.

"We didn't talk," I say, before I consider saying it.

"I didn't think you wanted to." He smiles down at me, rumpled pants, blue eyes. He doesn't look too much older than me, and his teeth are perfect. What kind of pervert would have perfect teeth?

He stares at me for a second, and though I know I'm supposed to say something, there's nothing I can say. I want to give this story a satisfying ending. I want to tell Clare and Jeannette all about my encounter with Mr. Stranger Danger, present them with an icky drippy condom, and have them go make a balloon. But there's nothing I can say to bring forth this happy ending, and instead I blink again, and force myself to speak.

"Have a good evening," I say. What?

"You too." He smiles at me, a great smile, perfect teeth, and walks off into the street. He has a bouncy walk.

I look at his back and wish he had some poetry to read to me on my answering machine. Then he would be my man. I should tell him this. I bound off the marble steps and into the night and the dark, cobblestoned streets. But once I keep running I just can't stop, and I pass him on the left. A queer shiver goes up me, starting from my legs and ending at my nose. I keep running.

"Hey!" I hear him call after me. "Where are you going?"

I might trip on an uneven pavestone, but I probably won't. I probably won't, in my jeans and my sneakers and my ponytail flying behind me. I feel like a woman who's narrowly escaped, who's running away from long red hair and long red nails and tight black dresses. I feel like a woman who refuses other people's leftovers, who does the rejecting, who knows what she wants and is willing to wait for every little bit of it. I am not running away. I'm running toward.

Or maybe I'm just scared.

But I haven't even gone that far, and I can still hear him behind me. "Hey," he calls again. "Hey, beautiful!"

Yellow Morning

CAITLIN'S MOTHER is dying and she wants me to be there for it. "The whiz-bang," she says. "The final act. Last curtain. Bells and whistles."

Caitlin's mother has cancer of the lungs, the bones, the breasts, the womb. Her death is going to be less a whiz-bang, more a sputtering out. We've known this for a while.

"It'll be a party," Caitlin says. "We'll get a cake."

Caitlin's always been like this, long as I've known her, making a huge deal out of the small things and acting like the biggest things in the world are of no particular importance. When she was sixteen, she lost her virginity to Bobby Hayes in his father's garage and didn't shut up about it for two weeks. Bobby Hayes, the boy *I* had a crush on. Oh, she said, it felt so good, didn't hurt at all like they said it would, she thought maybe she even came, it's possible. But then

Bobby Hayes didn't keep his mouth shut about it, and one day after school, two seniors were waiting for Caitlin by the back entrance to her house. They each did it to her in the backyard, pushed her head down to the base of the swing set, covered her mouth with their fat sweaty palms. She laughed about it later. Said word must have gotten around about what a good ride she was. That was all she said, but still I couldn't stay mad at her about screwing Bobby.

And now her mother's dying and Caitlin wants to get a cake. I asked her what kind. She said, Chocolate layer.

We were best friends and next-door neighbors all through growing up—our bedrooms faced each other's and we had all those stupid girly things, languages we shared and different codes that we'd beam to each other at night with a flashlight. If I flashed her three times quickly, it meant that I was ditching school the next day and she should too. If she flashed back three times quickly, it meant okay. We'd ditch about once a month, take the bus to the mall and sit at the food court, eat Wendy's and Chick-fil-A and smoke Capri cigarettes. This was back when you could smoke in the food court.

After high school, I went to Trenton State because my grades were all right and back then I had some thoughts about being a pediatrician or an architect. Caitlin stayed up in Hackensack, went to the community college for a few semesters but then dropped out and took a job at the Ann Taylor in Paramus, eight bucks an hour. She's been working there for six years already, and now she's the assistant manager and she gets a salary and benefits. She gets great clothing too, which is good, because for most of the time I've known her Caitlin hasn't been able to dress for shit.

So now I'm driving up through Maryland to get to Hackensack in time for Caitlin's mother to die. I didn't turn out to be a pediatrician or an architect; I'm a middle-school guidance counselor in Bethesda, right outside D.C. After college, I moved to the greater D.C. area to be with Danny, and we lived there together for a while. He was going to George Washington law school, a really smart guy, but fun. We had fun together. We met when he was a junior in college and I was a freshman, and he was my first and only real boyfriend, I guess. We stayed together for six years; he was the person who taught me to like sushi and five card stud and Bruce Willis movies. I haven't taken this drive without him in years.

I'm wearing a black blouse and black pants and black heels, even though it's tough to drive in heels, because I want to show some respect in case Caitlin's mother is dead by the time I get there. It could be any second, Caitlin said, on the phone with me this morning. Whiz-bang, she said. Sock it to me.

Well, all right.

In the twenty-odd years I knew Caitlin's mother, I never knew how to address her. It was just her and Caitlin in that house, and they were pretty informal with each other. Caitlin's mother smoked throughout dinner, and when dinner was over nobody said excuse me, or may I be excused. They just stood up, dumped the remains of dinner into the garbage, washed out their dishes, and went their separate ways. I always found their dinners amazing. In my house, four kids, dinner was a salad plus meat plus vegetable plus starch, and you didn't start eating until everyone said grace, and you didn't get up to leave until you asked to be excused. And we ate as a family, all six of us. It was such a fucking drag. Caitlin refused to eat at my house. She said she was always afraid she'd break something, screw something up.

Anyway, Caitlin's mother's name was, *is*—who can say right now if she's past tense or what?—Caitlin's mother's name is Mary Margaret Brody. She always told me to call her M.M., said that's what her friends called her, but I wasn't M.M.'s friend. Still, I couldn't call her Mrs. Brody, because she was adamant about not being a Mrs. anymore, and I couldn't call her Miss Brody, because that sounded so prissy and schoolteacherish. Most of the time I got around the problem by not addressing her at all—if I needed to get her attention, I'd clear my throat or cough. Caitlin called her mother "Maaaa!"

Caitlin came down to Bethesda eight months ago to talk about the fact that her mother, M.M., was starting to die. Danny took a break from the law books and we went out to Tio Pepe's for margaritas and grilled corn. "Cancer everywhere," Caitlin said, her long blond hair tied back from her face, her eyes sparkling blue. She was gripping the margarita with both hands, clearly excited. "It's amazing. It's like she's a big tomato with worms inside, you think she's all red and healthy when you look at her, but then you cut her open and she's totally rotten."

"Jesus," Danny said. He touched Caitlin's hand sympathetically. "You all right?"

"Sure," Caitlin said. "I mean, *I'm* not the one with cancer."

Danny and I had been having some problems at that point, and before Caitlin arrived we fought about where to put her. Our apartment had a pull-out couch but I thought it was only right to give Caitlin the bed. "Come on, Danny," I said. "Her mother's dying."

"I realize that," he said. "And I feel bad. But there isn't room for two people on the pull-out couch and just because we give her our bed doesn't mean we're going to save her mother's life."

"Jesus Christ!" I exploded. I'd never had a temper before the problems started with Danny. "Would it be so hard for you to *not* be an asshole for five minutes? She's my oldest fucking friend!"

We didn't talk to each other until Caitlin got there. When she did, she claimed she wouldn't *dream* of kicking us out of our room. No *way*. She didn't mind sleeper sofas at all, she said, they were totally comfortable, no problem. She was wearing a silky Ann Taylor shell and Ann Taylor trousers and she looked pretty together for a girl with a dying mother. I decided to believe her, that she really didn't mind about the couch.

After margaritas, Danny went to the law library to do some catching up and Caitlin and I went back home. I broke out a pack of Capri cigarettes I'd bought for the occasion and we sat up until two in the morning, drinking Bailey's, talking about nothing in particular. I asked her several times about her mother, the prognosis, what the doctors might be able to do. She kept going back to the tomato. "Once it's got worms," she said, "you just can't get 'em out. She's full of holes. I saw the MRI—she's a goddamn sponge."

A tomato, a sponge. I fell asleep that night, alone in the bed, and dreamt about fruits and vegetables.

I woke up around four in the morning; I needed water. All the drinking we'd done had left me pretty dehydrated. I crept out into the living room so as not to wake Caitlin and knew, even before I looked, what I was about to see. The knowing hit me like a brick, like a rock to the head. And yes, there. There he was—on top of her on the pull-out couch, moving up and down, moving quietly. I could hear Caitlin moaning underneath him and saying, "God, God, *more*."

I watched them for a minute or two. Then I went back to bed. For some reason, I never told Caitlin what I saw. I didn't know how to bring it up. But as for Danny—well, Danny I kicked out two days later. After Caitlin went back home to watch her mother die.

There's a rest stop on the Jersey Turnpike right after the Delaware Memorial Bridge that has yet to be colonized by Roy Roger's or Mickey D's. This far south in Jersey, the turnpike is still basically a four-lane road, not the ten-lane nightmare it becomes around Newark. I like to pull over here—it's a good halfway point between Bethesda and Hackensack, and the rest-stop diner makes a fairly decent cheeseburger. I get out of the car, twist my ankles around, bend down, and touch my toes. The June air is warm, breezy, and the sky is very blue. I think to myself that it doesn't seem like a bad day to die. Then I feel bad for thinking such terrible thoughts.

"Your best friend, huh," the guy says. "Well, I'm sorry to hear that."

"She's been sick for a long time," I say. "It's probably for the best."

"Now why do people say that?" the man says. He takes off his jacket, a dirty denim jacket, and rolls up the sleeves of his cotton shirt. His forearms are simply huge. "People like to say that when someone's been sick for a while. It's probably for the best, it's better this way. What a crock of shit." I look at him funny. "No matter what," he explains, "when you're sick you're still alive, but when you're dead, you're dead. There's still a little bit of hope in sick, but there's no hope whatsoever in dead."

"She had no hope," I say. "She had cancer everywhere. Like a tomato."

"Like a what?" the man says.

"Forget it," I say. I turn back to my food, find I'm losing my appetite.

"Listen," the man says. "I know you don't know me at all, I'm just a guy in a diner on the turnpike, you don't have to listen to me if you don't want. But I've been driving up from Florida for two days now to get my ass to Pittsburgh, and you're the prettiest thing I've seen since I've hit the road. I think you should skip the death watch and come on out with me. We'll have a couple of beers, see where the day takes us. You ever been to Pittsburgh?"

I smile at him. I like being told I'm pretty. "I have not," I admit. "But I don't even know your name."

"I'm Chris," he says. He sticks out a big paw for me to

I sit down at the Formica counter in the diner; it's one in the afternoon but I'm the only customer in the place. A waitress, a real Jersey-style waitress, stands behind the counter with a pencil tucked in her hair. She's snapping gum, just like in the movies.

"What'll you have, hon?" she asks me. Even though I know it's just waitress-speak, I really like it when strangers call me "hon."

"A cheddarburger," I say. "Medium well. And a cup of coffee."

"Fries?" she asks me.

"Extra crispy."

Growing up in Jersey, I spent so much time in diners that I know all their menus by heart, all the terminology. The Happy Waitress. The Monte Cristo sandwich. Sloppy onions. Sloppy onions with cheese. All these foods you wouldn't dream of eating anywhere else, you wouldn't even consider cooking for yourself. Caitlin's favorite was the Yellow Morning, which was a poached egg balanced on slices of sausage and surrounded by mashed potatoes. It actually looked all right. But once you touched the egg with the sharp end of your fork, it would split open and turn yellow and the whole damn thing would fall apart.

After my brother Joe left for college, I inherited his baby blue Civic and Caitlin and I would drive to the diners in Oradell, Westwood, Closter. During the summers, we'd take the Civic down to the shore and cover ourselves with Nivea Tan—I'd turn golden and Caitlin would get bright pink. Then, around five o'clock, we'd go to the Loveladies Diner and order the fried seafood platter with french fries and afterward drive home slowly, warm and full. Caitlin's mother would be waiting for us in her kitchen, smoking, drinking Sanka. "You ladies have fun today?" she'd ask us, her gray-blond hair in curlers, her fat legs wrapped in sweatpants. "Pick up any boys?"

"Maaa!"

"Listen, if I could still wear a bikini, I'd be right down there with you. I'd be picking up all the boys myself."

"Maaa!"

I loved it. My own mother had no idea I wore a bikini, since I kept mine in one of Caitlin's drawers. My own mother thought I wore the navy blue Speedo she bought me for gym class in the fall. My own mother was such a prude, it was embarrassing. I told Caitlin that I thought it must be cool to have M.M. for a mom, but she just rolled her eyes at me and told me not to be a moron. "Chutes and ladders," she said to me. "Dollars and donuts." She would say this sort of nonsense whenever she felt weird.

And now the waitress slaps down my cheddarburger with its sad little pickle and its sad little cup of coleslaw and a big side of dark brown fries. I love diner coleslaw. I love diner pickles. I eat with big, sloppy noises, since it's been a long time since I've been to New Jersey and I'm starting to feel like I'm home.

"Enjoying that, huh?" says a voice to my right.

I finish chewing, swallow. I wipe my lips. A burly-looking guy has taken the seat next to me, and he's smiling like he's just been really clever.

"Yes," I say. "I'm enjoying it a great deal."

"Where you headed to?" he asks me. He's kind of not [l]ooking, actually, not as cute as Danny but sort of charm[ing] anyhow, with freckles and big brown eyes.

"North Jersey," I say. "Hackensack."

"A funeral?" he asks me.

"Huh?" I grab at my coffee cup. "How'd you know?"

"All the black," he says to me, and smiles again.

The waitress brings him his own cup of coffee and [he] takes a big swill of it, like he's doing a shot. He's got en[or]mous hands. "I'm going to Pittsburgh, myself," he sa[ys]. "Gonna cut across to the Pennsylvania pike at exit six. G[et] out of here before Jersey gets all ugly on me."

"What's in Pittsburgh?" I ask, since I don't really mi[nd] talking to strangers.

"The usual bullshit," the burly man says. "Cheap beer. [I] got some old navy buddies up there and a few vacation da[ys], and they said Pittsburgh's not so bad anymore, or at least th[e] beer's still cheap." He sniggers. "We're gonna chase dow[n] some women, shoot some pool."

"Sounds like fun," I say.

"Too bad you've got a funeral," the burly guy says. H[e] takes another gulp of his coffee. "You coulda come along."

I nod at him, shrug, and turn back to my burger. There['s] such a thing as too friendly. I take a couple bites and stay quiet. For a few minutes, he does too.

Then he breaks the silence. "So who died?"

"What?" I say. "Oh, nobody yet. My best friend's mother, she's pretty sick. I mean she's dying. She could go at any minute."

shake, which I do, and his shake is nice enough, friendly. It occurs to me that I should find him more threatening than I do. "And what's your name?" he asks.

I tell him, and he repeats it, a smile spreading across his mouth. "That's nice," he says to me, and I'm starting to blush.

We talk for a little while, about Pittsburgh and the things to do there, about Hackensack and how there's really nothing to do *there*. In Pittsburgh, it seems, there's a great steak restaurant that just opened, steaks as good as you can get in New York City but for half the price and none of the attitude. He's really looking forward to that, he says. On the Gulf Coast of Florida, Chris eats a lot of fish he catches himself. He's a sport fisherman on the weekends. Come weekdays, he works for the water company. He left the navy five years ago. He seems pretty pleased with his arrangements.

Chris wants to know about Caitlin, about how long I've known her and what her mother is like, was like, and what Caitlin's going to do without her.

"Jesus," I say. "Those are tough questions. I mean, I really don't know. Caitlin was born in that house," I say. "She and her mom have lived there together for as long as I've known them."

"And that's been a while, huh?"

I do the math in my head. "Twenty-two years," I say.

"No shit," Chris says, and burps quietly.

When Caitlin called this morning, it was six-thirty and the sun had only just started coming up. I was awake, reading the paper. It's been hard for me to sleep the past eight months, ever since Danny's been gone. The usual things, you know. The bed feels empty, the apartment feels so empty. I don't buy enough food to fill up the fridge. Nobody makes coffee in the morning unless I feel like making coffee, which I never do. I feel like drinking it, but not making it, so I don't drink coffee at home anymore. Weekends I'll see the few friends I've got, or sometimes go to the movies, but I look for Danny everywhere. On busy streets, on the Metro, at Tio Pepe's, or in the Red Bear Bar. I've thought about calling him a lot, lately. I know how to find where he lives.

On the phone, six-thirty this morning, Caitlin was relieved to know she hadn't woken me. "It's today," she said. "You've got to come *today*."

School had ended last week and there was really nothing stopping me. "Is this it?" I asked. Taking Caitlin's cue, I was starting to treat her mother's death like a social event.

"You bet," Caitlin said. "The hospice nurse is here, she's taking my mother off the tubes. Mom's been slipping in and out of a coma for like two days now, and the nurse just thinks it's time. The doctor's gonna be here any second. This is *it*," Caitlin said. "She's going, going, gone."

"I'll be there as soon as I can," I said, and that's when Caitlin told me about the cake she was planning on. The chocolate layer.

We hung up. Then, even though I knew I should hurry, I just could not bring myself to rush. I made some tea, took a bath, spent a long time cleaning the apartment, scrubbing the bathroom, washing the tiles. I straightened up my underwear drawer. I packed carefully for four whole days, three days longer than I was planning on staying—jeans, skirts, T-shirts, a silk blouse. I called my own parents, long since retired to Arizona, and told them about Mary Margaret Brody. They both sent along their regrets.

Finally, around ten-thirty, I headed out onto the highway. I didn't call Caitlin before I left, like I had promised to do. I didn't break the speed limits on the roads.

Chris is looking at me all serious while I tell him this. His brown eyes seem shiny with concern. "Nobody's got a gun to your head," he says, after a minute. "You don't gotta go to Jersey if you don't want to."

"That," I tell him, picking up and then putting down a fry, "is where you're wrong."

"Come on out to Pittsburgh with me," Chris says again. "I'm not kidding. You'll like it. You'll see."

"Hey," I say, as the waitress refills both our coffee mugs. "Hey, Mr. Invite, why don't you come with me? Screw Pittsburgh. Come meet my best friend's dead mother in New Jersey. You'll love Hackensack," I say, trying to sound all sarcastic. "We'll have a real good time."

"Hell," Chris says. He picks up his coffee mug, takes a long, slow sip. He's stopped swilling. "There ain't no fun in funeral," he says after a while.

Which is something like what Danny said about Caitlin. "That girl," he said. "She wants to put the fun back into funeral."

Well, after all. Whiz-bang, Caitlin had said on the phone. Oh, the crazy times. And a cake, of all things—a fucking cake. As I stare down at the remains of my cheeseburger, it occurs to me that Caitlin doesn't even like chocolate. Never has. My stomach twists. "Excuse me," I say, and rush to the back of the diner. In the vestibule next to the bathrooms, I punch my calling-card number into a payphone. Four rings, five, six. Finally, Caitlin's voice.

"Where are you?" she asks, weakly.

"What's going on?"

"Two hours ago," Caitlin says. "Two hours." There's no more excitement in her voice, no more bells or whistles. "They took out the tubes and then she opened her eyes and then she closed them. She didn't say anything." I'm hearing something strange, unfamiliar, and I realize that for the first time in twenty-two years, I'm listening to Caitlin cry.

"I'm so sorry," I say.

"I know," she says. "Please get here soon."

Back at the counter, Chris is taking out his wallet, counting out the bills inside. I sit back down next to him, close my eyes, rest my head on my fists. I think of Caitlin's mother. I hope that she wasn't in too much pain.

"So you're off to Hackensack?" Chris asks. He's depositing a five-dollar bill on the counter, even though coffee here probably costs seventy-five cents.

"Yeah," I say, my head still on my fists. "Her mother died a few hours ago."

"I'm sorry about that," Chris says. "I guess you gotta do it then, right? No cheap beer for you, missy."

"No," I say. The waitress has cleared away my plate, and

all that's left on the counter is a balled-up napkin and a grease stain. It feels like hours since I walked into this place.

"Listen," Chris says. "You ever come down to the Gulf Coast, you look me up. I'll take you fishing, show you a good time." He takes a piece of paper out of his wallet. On it's his name and number, already scribbled out. For emergencies, I think to myself. "You look like you could use a vacation, anyway," Chris says.

"I guess I could," I say. It's all that comes to mind.

Chris nods at me and then cuffs me gently on the shoulder. He walks toward the door of the diner in a real slow manner, and I watch him go, with his dirty denim jacket and his broad shoulders and his tight ass in old khaki pants. Although he isn't shaped like Danny, watching him reminds me of that manly walk, that wonderful walk, the walk of men who know where they're going. I haven't stared at a man's ass like this in quite a while. For a selfish second, I think about what took Danny away from me. And I think of Pittsburgh and all those good times, and I think of Hackensack, a place for the dead and the gone.

Caitlin didn't call for a while after her visit to Bethesda. When she finally did, I told her that Danny and I had broken up. She was quiet for a moment, and then she started talking her old nonsense. "Sticks and fiddlers," she said to me. "That fucking sucks, really."

"It does," I agreed.

She changed the subject to her mother, white blood cells, radiation therapy. What could I say? My own heart, though empty, was healthy, at least, and probably destined to continue beating for forty or fifty more years. I didn't mention Danny again; it seemed beside the point.

But Caitlin sent me a card a week later, one of those not-so-funny Hallmark things, a card from the Just Between Us Girls line. On the inside, she'd scribbled: "Roses are red, Violets are blue, Men are useless, and you didn't need him in the first place." I held the card over the stove and burned it on an open flame. I can see the card now, white and orange and red, turning to dusty ash in my fingers.

"Chris," I say before I think about what I'm saying. He's still by the door, lighting a cigarette out of the wind. "I'm coming with you."

He turns around and smiles, a decent man's smile on a big brawny face. "Nah," he says. "What about Hackensack? The funeral?"

"They don't have cheap beer in Hackensack," I say, and try for a smile of my own. "What I mean is . . . "

"Hey," Chris says. He inhales on his cigarette, shrugs slightly. "You don't have to explain."

"Thanks," I say, and put a ten-dollar bill on the counter. I pick up my purse, sling it over my shoulder, and nod at my new friend. "I'm coming with you," I repeat, to reinforce it.

"You probably shouldn't," he says, after a second and another shrug. "What I mean is, your friend needs you. Anyway, let's face it, it's just Pittsburgh. I mean Pittsburgh's probably not the greatest shakes. And you've got your friend."

"But I thought—" I start, and then sit back down on the stool, unsure how to finish. What I'm thinking is, Caitlin's taken another one from me.

"Hey," he says again, before he turns around to leave. "I mean it about Florida. Give me a call if you ever come down."

I don't answer, and in a moment I hear the door behind him swing shut. So there's nothing keeping me in this diner anymore. But Chris is right—there's probably not much to head for in Pittsburgh, either. And when I think about it, what exactly do I have back home? Hackensack is where I should be headed. I should get up and go now, I suppose. But instead I just sit where I am. A few minutes later, I ask the waitress for another cup of coffee.

John on the Train: A Fable for Our Cynical Friends

HE WAS A REPORTER at *Men's Image* magazine, writing pieces about biceps and the new trendy styles in boxer-briefs. He looked like a reporter, too, or what he imagined the archetype reporter should look like: glasses, sandy thinning hair, white button-down shirt. A genial sort of invisibility, a face that, while it wouldn't offend, certainly wouldn't last too long in anyone's memory. Most of the men who worked at *Men's Image* looked a lot like John, but most of them thought they looked better.

In order to get to work in the morning, John left his apartment in Astoria, Queens—a large studio with nothing on the walls and nothing in the refrigerator—and took the R train to Fifty-seventh Street, where he would disembark, buy a dry bagel and a cup of coffee, and be in his cubicle by

10:15. This pattern rarely changed. John was, in general, resistant to change—he'd worn the same style of glasses since the ninth grade.

And so it was on a Wednesday, a sunny Wednesday at the tail end of March, when the Greek butcher shops were beginning to advertise whole goats to buy for Easter, and the windowsills turned red with Easter flowers, that John walked three blocks to the R train and sat down on a worn brown bench to wait. He didn't read on the subway, because every journal and periodical he might want was kept at work under his desk, and anyway, he used his time on the train to close his eyes, to reflect, to think. He thought usually about his plans to leave *Men's Image* any day now, and go find a real job with a real newspaper, one whose goals and subjects he could respect. Maybe the *New York Times*. Maybe the *Wall Street Journal*.

And on this Wednesday, this aforementioned sunny March Wednesday, John heard the train rumble and opened his eyes and stood up and brushed off any bench-dirt from his khakis, and made sure his leather bag was secure around his shoulder, and turned to look for the train. And saw her.

(Looking back on this moment in future hours, days, or years, John couldn't explain what it was about her exactly that he fell in love with in the time it takes an R train to roll into the Steinway Street station. She was beautiful, yes, but John was suspicious of beauty and didn't expect or demand it of himself or others. Her clothing was ordinary: corduroy pants, a black sweater, a black wool coat. Sneakers. Her head was bent, graceful, poring over the *Times*, and when John stood behind her to get on the train he saw she was reading the *Dining In/Dining Out* section, which pleased him greatly. But why her? Why love? Why this Wednesday? You could ask John today; he still wouldn't be able to tell you exactly other than to say that it was there.)

John felt his stomach plummet. He wanted to throw up. If this was love, and he knew when she turned and smiled at him that it was, it must be—well, then, he didn't like it. He had heard of love's side effects, of course: nervousness, sweats, the compulsion to sit by the phone and wait for it to ring regardless of any other activity the evening might present. But he hadn't realized that nausea was part of the package. John hated nausea. But she smiled at him—it was an honest-to-God smile!—and John was helpless with illness and joy. What a state.

He sat across from her and watched her read. She was good at folding the *Times* without getting it in anyone's face, and he could see that her nails were short and painted pink, and her skin was clear and also pink, and that some of her hair had escaped its ponytail and fell curly around her face. John felt even more nauseated, and she must have sensed his nausea, or perhaps even his love, as they radiated from him in waves of equal power; she looked up at him and, again, she smiled.

John turned away, his face fire-purple, his heart beating madly, madly.

When she got off the train at Lexington Avenue, John palmed the subway glass like a lost child, watching her hips move under her long wool coat as the train pulled him away.

He got off two stops later and forgot to buy his bagel.

"You," Andy said. They had adjoining cubicles and matching iMac computers. "What's the matter with you today? You're not acting right in the head. You're not acting like yourself."

John turned to Andy. He had been writing the same sentence all day, in different permutations: "There's nothing women like more than a gleaming shaved head."

Or: "Nothing turns on a woman like the strength and masculinity of a shaved head."

Or: "Shave your head. It'll get you laid."

"Andy," John said, running a hand through his own thinning hair. "Do you think I should shave my head?"

"Shave your head?" Andy said. Andy was one of the better-looking staffers at *Men's Image*, and liked to leave cocktail napkins on his desk with women's numbers scrawled on them. "Nah—I don't think so. Chicks don't like that so much."

"No?" John said. "But what if you're balding anyway?"

"Hmmph," Andy said, and touched his scalp as if to check. "Well, I wouldn't know anything about that."

John put his head in his hands, closed his eyes, and thought about this brown-haired, brown-eyed, black-wooled girl, and remembered and tried to feel again the brief electric shock that passed between his hand and the edge of her coat as he walked behind her boarding the R train. He wondered if she lived in Astoria and, if so, why he had never seen her there before. How could he have missed her? And yet he hadn't seen her before, he was sure of it, because if he had he would have noticed her and fallen in love on some other day before today.

And so he decided she must be new to the neighborhood, new to Steinway Street, and this could be her first day of a new commute. But who moves during the week? Wouldn't her first day of a new commute be a Monday? So maybe she wasn't new to the area. However maybe she decided to go in late today for some reason. Or maybe, just maybe she wasn't in a work uniform, no pearls—so maybe she was a student. Maybe she was heading off to class. Or maybe she had decided to take the day off and was just heading into the city to go shopping. Or to go to a museum. She seemed like the museum type.

"Hey," Andy called again. "What's the matter with you?"

"Oh," John said, slightly embarrassed. "It's just—it's nothing."

John sat in his cubicle until eight-thirty, but he got very little done that day.

The next morning, John woke up at six without the assistance of either an alarm clock or the cacophony of drunks who shrieked all night, every night, on his corner. It was already sunny out. He hadn't realized that insomnia, too, was one of the side effects of love.

He had dreamt about her.

He was troubled by this, that he had dreamt about her, because he'd been fairly sure that it was just a twelve-hour case of love, nothing to get too worked up about, take two aspirin and call me in the morning. He expected to wake up the next day perhaps a little worse for wear, but in better spirits generally and more alert. He certainly hadn't expected to feel worse.

John had dreamt that they were on the subway platform. She was wearing her wool coat, her hair was pulled back off her face, and tiny hoops glittered in her ears. She didn't notice that he was thin, sandy-haired, nondescript. She smiled at him again. She said, "John, I've been waiting."

"What have you been waiting for?" he asked. "How did you know my name?"

She smiled. "I've been waiting for what we've all been waiting for, you dummy." She stood closer to him, and he dreamt her warm breath and the sweet, slightly pepperminty smell of her hair and coat and skin.

"Dummy?" John asked, and even in his dream he felt faint.

Then the train pulled into the station, and he got on, and she got on, but it was a crowded train and she disappeared in the crowd. John looked for her, walked up and down the car, peered into faces over newspapers, bumped into commuters and old people and homeless people, and then changed cars, looking for her, the subway air heavy and thick, the bright orange seats as shiny as glass. He walked down the train, through every car, subway ads and dirt on the floors and gum on the floors and people, the wrong people.

At the end of the train, at the very last car, there she sat, folding her newspaper. When he approached her, she looked up. "You found me," she said.

"I found you," he said. And woke up.

At eight in the morning, John looked in the mirror. He seemed to have lost some hair overnight. He was stubbly, he was pale, he had circles under his eyes. "Shit," John thought to himself. "I look like shit."

It was still early. John put on his sneakers and went running through the streets of Astoria. Every house he passed, every apartment building, every face in a bakery or a butcher shop, John imagined was hers. She bought her flowers here. She bought bagels and coffee at this bodega. Or this one. An old lady swept her driveway in a blue housecoat, a cigarette dangling from her lips. That's her grandmother, John thought to himself. She lives here with her grandmother.

He ran faster.

He passed the bank with the clock for a sign and saw that it was almost nine. He had been running for close to an hour, but he felt no cramps, no tight muscles. He wasn't out of breath. There was another bakery next to the bank, and its door was open. He smelled coffee cake, blueberry muffins.

He had to get ready for work.

But the thought of getting dressed, of going down to the subway—what if she wasn't there? What if she *was* there? He would be equally miserable in either case. If he didn't see her again, then he would miss her, wonder what happened, wonder if he'd ever get to see her again and, if not, how he would get over his sickening case of love and his nausea. But if she was there, that might be worse. What would he say to her? How could he explain himself? And if he said nothing, well, what if she figured out he was a coward? Nobody falls in love with a coward.

He thought briefly about taking the bus.

John got up, walked around his studio, looked again in the mirror. The run had brightened his cheeks a bit, and the circles under his eyes seemed diminished. "Well," he said out loud to himself. "Well, that's a little bit better."

He took a shower, shaved, and put on khaki pants and a white button-down shirt. He wondered if he should buy some new clothes. He wondered if he should move out of Queens. As he laced up his sneakers he thought of a plan: I will sit there, he thought, and I will wait for three trains to pass. If she comes, then I will say hello to her, or nod at her, or say nothing at all, but whatever I choose to do I will not regret later. If she does not come, then I will get on the fourth train, and go to work, and stop behaving like a complete idiot.

He walked the three blocks to the Steinway Street station and tried not to be nervous and tried not to be nauseated. He told himself that rationally there was no reason for her to show up again. He had never seen her there before; moreover, how many times does a person see another person on the subway and then never see that person again? All the time. That's the usual way it goes.

He walked into the coolness and darkness of the Steinway Street station and passed the Jews for Jesus handing out leaflets and passed the old Pakistani man selling newspapers and passed the token vendor selling Metrocards. He swiped his Metrocard. He felt the back of his neck become irrationally sweaty.

He walked down the stairs to the platform and sat down on the worn wooden bench and heard the approaching train rumble in the distance. "No!" John thought to himself. "Train number one cannot pass yet! You haven't given her any time!"

But he stood up anyway, because he felt like a fool waiting for a stranger in a subway station in Queens, and because if he let this train pass, and then another one, there was nothing to say that he wouldn't sit in the station all day, waiting for her to show up.

And so, pretending that today was just another day, because it was—wasn't it really?—John stood up, and brushed off any bench-dirt from his khakis, and made sure his leather bag was secure around his shoulder, and turned to look for the train. And again, he saw her.

The black wool coat. The brown hair, still tied back off her face. Her neck, white, curved, and the side of her face as she read the *New York Times*. John felt his cheeks get hot. The air around him grew thick.

The words, "Hey, there!" in bright tones of anxiety, enthusiasm, hope burst from his mouth before he could stop them.

She turned and smiled again, that vicious, stomach-wracking smile. "Hi," she said, and her voice was low and soft. And then the train opened its greasy mechanical doors, and she disappeared inside of them, and John had no choice but to follow.

He couldn't look at her. Looking at her made his face too hot and his stomach too twisted—and the words *hey there, hey there* kept circling round his brain like riders on a Ferris Wheel. John stared at the ad for cut-rate dermatology posted above her head and felt her glance at him every once in a while. He didn't dare look down to meet her eyes. He prayed his face wasn't as purple as he was quite sure that it was.

At 59th Street/Lexington Avenue, she said, "Have a nice day." She was looking at him, her paper in her hand, a black canvas bag slung across her shoulders. Her eyes weren't brown—they were goldish green.

"You too," John bargled, and watched again, helpless, as she disappeared outside the subway doors.

"You," Andy said. He was wearing a baseball cap. "You look worse."

"I know," John said. "I got up too early."

"Really?" Andy raised a single eyebrow, a trick that he was good at. "Any particular reason? Someone kick you out of bed?"

"Oh," John said, and scratched his nose. "Not exactly."

Andy chuckled. "You are a lonely man, John my friend. You spend too much time alone. You should come out with me this weekend. I could introduce you to some nice ladies."

John nodded.

"You do like the ladies, don't you, John? I mean, in general, in terms of affection, it is the ladies that you like, right?"

"Sure, Andy," John said, turning back to his computer. "I like the ladies."

This was true. It was the ladies, in terms of affection, that John liked, even though he hadn't seen one naked in over two years. Before that, back when he'd lived in the heartland, even back when he'd attended the state college, John saw ladies both clothed and unclothed on a relatively regular basis. John used to go out with them and buy them beers or listen to their tapes of the Grateful Dead. But then, restless, John decided to leave the heartland and move to New York, where things weren't as easy, where the women wore black and talked too fast and demanded, John thought, an awful lot.

They had warned him that New York was dangerous, which it really wasn't, but also admitted grudgingly that New York might be fun, which it could be sometimes. What they hadn't told him was that New York was expensive, unbelievably expensive, although most New York jobs paid little more than their counterparts paid in the heartland. And so John didn't have the money to take out the fast-talking women, and he didn't have the confidence of cool new shoes or a great apartment or perhaps the occasional Knicks ticket. John didn't have the swagger or the temperament of a true New Yorker, and his colleague Andy was right. John was sometimes a lonely man.

"Come on out with me, buddy," Andy said. "Come on out this weekend. Oh, the fun we'll have."

John nodded and touched his sandy hair.

He got home at a quarter to nine and put the mail on the large kitchen table, which was also his desk, which was also where he kept paperback novels and his collection of baseball caps. There was a letter from his mother, a not uncommon thing, requesting that he come home at least for a visit and maybe to stay. His father had been ill. Jenny Loomis, old high-school girlfriend, was getting married. Linda Porter had had a wonderful time on her trip to Hawaii and brought back macadamia nuts for John's family, which was certainly good news. And also, everyone missed him. John put down the letter and thought, I do not want to go back.

Besides the letter, there were other things in the mail. Bills, for example, to which John would attend later, and a copy of *TV Guide*, which he was slightly embarrassed to receive but which came free with his cable subscription. He sighed and cracked open the window above the kitchen table. On nights like this, permeated with an unfocused sense of longing and a feeling of general uselessness, John often smoked a little marijuana and watched televised football, or called old friends from the heartland to see how things went on the farm or at the auto dealer or with the new baby. But tonight, John's head felt too clogged for marijuana, it wasn't yet football season, and he didn't feel like making a phone call. He put his feet on the table and thought about the girl on the train. He wondered what her name was.

When the phone rang, John jumped, startled out of what was turning into a very nice daydream, slightly erotic.

"Yes?" John asked. "Hello?"

"John? It's Andy! You've got to come out tonight! I'm here on the East Side, I'm at a bar! I'm with some lovely ladies, John, you gotta come. I won't take no for an answer."

John smiled at his reflection in the window above the kitchen table. He thought that it was sweet, if a little peculiar, that Andy was so dedicated to improving a co-worker's social life. "I don't know, man. I'm pretty beat."

"It's at—hold on—what's the address here?" Andy yelled out. The bar behind him sounded noisy and crowded. "It's at—" Andy shouted the address. "I'll see you in half an hour." He hung up.

John chuckled, still cradling the phone next to his ear. Ordinarily he didn't like to go out much to bars, especially on weeknights, when the post-work crowd hustled each other and fought for a place at the counter to order seven-dollar gin and tonics. Bars on the East Side, especially, were notorious for that sort of scene, stuffed from banquette to bartender with cheesy music and investment bankers. Fast talkers. On the other hand, it wasn't yet basketball season, and John wasn't as tired as he'd protested. A new blue shirt hung in his closet, and some cologne was on his dresser, and a little company might not be a bad idea. Andy would be pleased.

The Astoria night was warm, and the Arab men who owned the bodega under John's apartment were sitting on boxes outside, smoking. John had bought orange juice and toilet paper from these men for two years; they were neighborly. "Hey," they said to him as he walked outside.

"Hey," John said. "Could I bum a cigarette?" He liked to smoke the occasional cigarette. Smoking burned his throat and made his eyes water, but when he felt nervous or edgy it helped him breathe in, breathe out.

He stood quietly with the Arab men, smoking his cigarette, watching Greek girls in pretty dresses walk up and down the sidewalk, their boyfriends shouting on cell phones or talking to them in low voices. A tricked-out Pontiac Firebird, white, with dice hanging from the rearview mirror, cruised slowly down the street. At the wheel was a dark-haired girl with glasses and John thought for a moment—but no. When this girl turned to look at John, he saw that her eyes were too narrow, her nose was too pug. It could not be the girl from the train, and he was relieved, because he didn't want to think of the girl from the train driving a cheesy, tricked-out Pontiac Firebird.

He stubbed out his cigarette.

"You going out tonight, my friend?" One of the Arab men, the kindly balding one who sold him his Sunday *Times*, was leaning back against the plate-glass window of the shop, smiling at John.

"Yeah, out with a friend. Some bar in Manhattan."

"You go out with your girlfriend?"

"No, no . . . just some guy from work."

"Aah," the man said, his smile unchanged. "Well, you go have good time. In the morning I sell you aspirin, whatever you need."

John nodded his thanks and headed towards Steinway.

The place was called Divine Bar, on East Fifty-second Street. It was a narrow room with wood floors and a long marble bar, and a crowd medium in number sat in low velvet couches, or at stools along the marble bar, or stood up talking with their friends.

"I met the most delicious lady here last weekend," Andy said.

"Delicious?" John asked. "Really?"

"Took me home and did things you only see in the movies, Johnny," Andy said, as they settled themselves on stools. "Turns out she was married—her husband was away on business. Always away on business, she said. I told her next time your husband's away on business, I'll make it *my* business to come on over and keep you a little company."

"Married," John said. He didn't want to find a lady who was married. He didn't want to find a lady in Divine Bar. He wanted the girl on the train, whom he didn't know at all but whom he still knew wouldn't be here.

The bartender gave them two Coronas, and Andy slipped her a twenty, and when John tried to pay him back Andy laughed and pushed the money away. "This is your night, my friend. The beer's on me."

John nodded and looked away. Until two girls in tight black pants crowded in from behind them at the bar, nothing more was said.

"And what do we have here?" Andy asked. One of them, the taller one, was trying to catch the bartender's eye. "I'll take care of that," Andy said to the girl, and waved his hand at the bartender.

Their names were Tracy and Paula, and Andy claimed Paula, the taller one, by standing up and offering her his barstool. John realized he should offer Tracy his barstool, but as he stood she said, "Don't bother. I like to stand."

"Okay," John said, and settled himself back down and then wondered whether or not he should have insisted.

She wasn't pretty, nor was she ugly. She was smooth, bland, pale. Her yellow hair fell straight, like paper, to her shoulders. "So what do you do?" she asked, sipping her Rolling Rock.

"I'm a reporter," John said.

She nodded. "That's pretty cool," she said. "I'd like to get into reporting myself, maybe. I've always sort of seen myself on television."

"Television?" John asked.

"Or something like that," she said. "I'm in sales now," she said. "Where do you do your reporting?"

"A magazine," John said. "It's for men."

"I read *Cosmopolitan*," Tracy offered. "I also read *Jane*."

"I'd like to work for the *New York Times*," John said. He'd had no idea what else to say and this was the first thing to occur to him.

"Who wouldn't?" Tracy asked. "I have to visit the restroom. I'll be right back."

As soon as Tracy was gone, Andy hit him in the back. Paula had vanished too, to accompany her friend. "What did I tell you, man? What did I say?"

"What did you say?" John asked.

"The ladies, you idiot!" Andy clinked his beer bottle against John's. "I told you I'd introduce you to some nice ladies. What do you think? Pretty hot, huh?"

"Pretty hot," John agreed, because it was easier to agree than to explain to Andy why he didn't. He unbuttoned his top button and cracked his wrist and looked at Andy again, closer.

When they returned, Paula stood close to Andy and Tracy stood close to John. He asked her about sales (boring) and where she was from (Philadelphia) and where she lived right now (an East Village walk-up with her brother). The conversation didn't flow; it jerked in fits and starts, and several times John noticed Tracy's eye wander across the bar to assess, he assumed, the other prospects.

Finally, after one more beer apiece and an apologetic tug at her friend Paula's blouse, Tracy excused herself. "It's late," she said. "I have a sales conference tomorrow."

"Of course," John said, relieved. "Nice to meet you."

They disappeared through the crowded bar, and Andy hit John on the arm. Always hitting, John thought. "Number?" Andy asked. "You get her number?" John shook his head, feeling like a bit of a failure. Andy motioned to the bartender for another beer. "Johnny," he said. "How can I help you if you refuse to help yourself?"

That night, John dreamt again that he was on the subway, but he was in a special car, the bar car. Waitresses in short skirts passed by carrying trays of cocktails: martinis, Manhattans, vodka tonics. John sat under a poster advertising STD awareness and watched the crowds mingle, drink and smoke and chatter, as the train moved at lightning speed through tunnels underground. Periodically it stopped at neon-lit stations, and new crowds got on and old crowds got off. Someone offered John a scotch and soda, and he took it, grateful.

"Aren't you gonna say thank you?" She was there, she was at this party on the train—her *New York Times* was folded under her arm.

"Thank you," John said. "I didn't expect you to be here."

"I know," the girl said, and smiled at him, her goldish-green eyes crinkling at the corners. "This isn't usually my scene. But I was feeling kind of restless tonight and thought it might be nice to go out."

"Will you be able to get to work tomorrow?"

"Oh yes," the girl said. "Don't worry. I'll be on the train tomorrow."

John paused. Then he said, finally, "Scotch and soda." He paused again. "My father drinks that."

"My father does too," the girl said. "Sometimes, when I lived at home, he'd make one for me and one for him and we'd watch Mets games together. I remember nineteen eighty-six," she said, "when the Mets won the World Series, I was fourteen, and to celebrate my dad made me a scotch and soda and we sat there together on the couch, happy and buzzed from the alcohol."

"Sounds like fun," John said.

"We still go to games together," the girl said.

"I'd like to take you to go see the Mets," John said. "I'd like to take you anywhere. We can drink scotch and soda together. "

"Let's get off," the girl said, and the train stopped suddenly.

They emerged under the bright lights of a baseball stadium, the seats packed full of screaming fans. In the bleachers sat Andy and Tracy and Paula, John's mother and father, the Arab guys from the bodega, his boss. He looked under his feet and saw sand and a smooth white base plate. They were standing at home base.

"Look at where we've found ourselves," the girl said, and she took John's hand, and together they waved to the crowd.

The crowd roared back in appreciation, congratulations, and John woke up smiling.

She was there again that morning, just like she'd promised. Because March had become warm in the strange and inviting way that March sometimes does, she was no longer wearing her black wool coat. She had on jeans, and a green sweater, and a fuzzy blue scarf tied around her neck. She was smiling.

"Hello," she said to John. "Nice to see you again." There was an Indian family on the platform near them, and the women's saris glittered yellow and pink. John looked at all the beautiful color there in the coolness and cement of the Steinway Street station. It occurred to him that bright color often appears in the most unexpected places.

He had known he would see her there this morning, and the fact that she spoke to him was also not an entire surprise. "It's nice to see you too," he said. His voice came easily. "Where's your paper?"

"Didn't buy one today," she said. "The Friday paper's so damn bulky. What do I need with two separate *Weekend* sections?"

"Did you just move here?" John said, even though this didn't follow necessarily from her criticism of the Friday *New York Times*.

She smiled at him. Her eyes crinkled at the corners the way they did in his dream. John felt his heart flutter, and the women's saris swirled and sparkled in his peripheral vision. "I did," she said. "Last week."

"Well, welcome to the neighborhood," John said, and then, because he felt courageous and warm, because she spoke slowly and smiled kindly and because it was time to do so, he said, "You ever go see the Mets?"

"What?" she said, and looked confused, but as John was about to blush or explain or pass out from the sudden rush of adrenaline, she corrected herself. "No," she said. "I know they're the local team and everything—Shea Stadium's not too far from here, right? But I've actually never been to a pro baseball game. Never seen the Mets play, or the Yankees, for that matter."

"Never been to a pro baseball game?" John said, and then remembered that he had never been to one either. "Me neither," John said, "but I was thinking of going. I'm sort of new here too, and I thought a baseball game might be a good— a good—" But he faltered. His luck might have run out.

It didn't; she rescued him. "A good introduction to Queens?"

"Yeah," John said, and smiled. His heart fluttered again. She was lovely.

"Well, if you ever want company on your way to a game, let me know," she said, rescuing him further. "I'd love to see the Mets play."

Saved! He felt like a champion. "I was hoping," he said, "that you would."

"My name's Kate," she said.

"I'm John," he said, and shook her thin white hand.

And then the train rumbled in the distance, and the women in saris lined up against the edge of the platform, their husbands standing behind them with thick turbans wrapped around their heads. John made sure his leather bag was secure around his shoulders, and turned to look for the train. Kate stood next to him, and as the train rushed into the station, her curls blew off her face.

They boarded behind the women in saris and the men in turbans, onto the grimy silver car with the burnt orange interior and the fast-food cartons on the floor and the drunk man asleep in the corner. It was amazing, how beautiful everything became. She sat down and patted the seat next to her, which he took. She smiled. And as the doors bumped shut, and the train chugged into a full roar, John smiled back, glad that during his second winter in the most dangerous and exciting city in the world, he had finally arrived in New York.

Acknowledgments

With gratitude and love, I would like to thank my family, especially Carolyn and Lester Edelstein and Hannah and Nat Grodstein. I would also like to express my appreciation to the inspiring faculty and students of the Columbia Writing Division, to Kate Kelly, Allison Jaffin, Seth Unger, and Jill Grinberg, who supported me from the very beginning, and to all the wonderful friends who listened, commiserated, cheered, and thought up ideas for the cover. Thanks also go to Gabe Fried for being both a great editor and a dear, dear person. And, finally, to Julie Barer, my kind and brilliant agent, therapist, and friend—thank you for being the best of all possible animals.